The Girl in the Mirror
Book 1

by P. Costa

DORRANCE
PUBLISHING CO
EST. 1920
PITTSBURGH, PENNSYLVANIA 15238

Dorrance Publishing Co.
585 Alpha Drive
Suite 103
Pittsburgh, PA 15238
Visit our website at www.dorrancebookstore.com

ISBN: 978-1-6376-4200-9
EISBN: 978-1-6376-4834-6

Dedication

Dedicated to my many Mothers - Nora June, Lena, Katherine, Artista, Elsie and Edna. All of you have contributed to my life in profound and quietly meaningful ways. Your influence helped me to become a better person.

This book is dedicated to all of our memories of love for each other. I am humbly grateful for all of you and your generous love.

In The Beginning

She did not know her beginning, but many others did, and they seemed to get such joy out of talking about it. They added to it, or changed it from time to time. It was new news each time, a tidbit into the sight you normally do not see in families. She felt sad hearing it. She soon became used to tuning out those who gossiped about her or her family.

Her Mother was criticized for having her. The ninth child, especially after having Tuberculosis, and spending so many years in the Sanitarium. It was sad really. They judged her Mother openly in conversations in the grocery store or the gas station parking lot. When she heard them, she clenched her teeth and fists tight.

It was a fast 8½ months, an easy pregnancy. Then suddenly there she was with hair of gold, and light eyes, almost blue. All five pounds and three ounces of her. Her Momma was delighted. The only girl out of nine children. She was a gift, a wish come true.

Poppa was a big man, slender, 5' 11" tall, and dark jet black hair. His word was law in their home. He never said much. All too often his hand connected with the back side of one of his children. And holler! Oh, dear, did he ever yell at them a lot. It was very frightening. Poppa was a hard man to understand. One minute he would be laughing and smiling. Soon after, angry smashing a board, or chasing after one or two of the kids with a belt in his hands.

Momma was opposite. Kind and quiet, sweet and good-natured. She was a small woman, 4' 11", but she was very strong. She had light auburn hair, and deep brown eyes. It was said she was Native American, from the Chippewa tribe. You could usually find her in the kitchen singing, or sewing, or perhaps in the barn with the cows. It was her job to do the milking. The animals responded to her kind touch.

When she was born, she was to be named Rose. This one was no rose. As her Momma thought about it, it was Springtime and the name April came to mind. It was then and there she became April.

Her name was fresh as a spring day, full of promise of what was to come. She loved her little girl, and as her hair grew, it was hues of yellow curls.

As a Mother she loved all her children, but she was grateful to have a girl. Someone who she could cook with, teach to sew, and all the other womanly things that a Mother hopes to share with her daughter. She found such joy thinking about all of the things they would do together as she grew. Helping her with her grandchildren, as they were born. Sharing recipes, and time, time spent together. As she held her, she felt uneasy, as if time would elude her. She shook her head and dismissed the nonsense feelings. April was here to stay. She would do everything in her power to hold onto this little one, she was hers.

But Poppa refused to hold her, not ever! He always had excuses. He was busy, and there were always things to do. She was always underfoot, always needing something - girl's clothing, girl's shoes, girl's hair things. And there were tests, always tests. Trips to the hospital, time after time. It was always alarming if there was any reaction to the TB tests. April was always a nuisance and a problem. That is how her Poppa saw her, nothing more.

Most of her siblings tolerated her. She was too young to do any work, and just got in their way. Her siblings ranged in age from seven to twenty-one years. The youngest two brothers were her closest friends.

Tim was eight and John seven. Tim was a tall skinny boy with glasses. He would tilt his head to the side when he spoke, as if he were in the bright light of the sun. His nature was quiet and gentle. He loved to tinker with small mechanical things, and put models together. He handled her with the same patience and gentle guidance as he did with the models he built with pride.

The other brother, John, had a genuine sense of devilish humor. It was nothing for him to jump on a rail, and balance himself as carefully as he could to impress her. Or to make her laugh. He loved to color beside her, and read books to her. Not the fairy tale books, but the exciting books of pirates and cowboys in duels. He loved to see her face squish up. Sometimes she would close her eyes, and he would laugh at her.

It was these two, who kept her out of the watchful eye of their father. And it was also these two who received spankings with their father's leather belt and buckle. To them it was of utmost importance to keep their little sister safe, no matter what. They dutifully would stand there and take the undeserved punishment like little men, which they were proud to do. They would grit their teeth, close their eyes tight, and think of happy things.

"It doesn't hurt too bad," John once said to her as she saw the bright red belt marks on his legs and backside. She was not supposed to see that. She was almost three years old, and Momma told her to give the boys privacy. As he was getting out of the bathtub, April saw the bruises. She could not take her eyes off of those welts.

After he got out, it was her turn to go in. She sat in that bathtub unable to move, unable to wash. She just sat there and cried. She asked aloud, "Why, why do we have to live this way? Why can't we just be nice and kind like they are to me? Why are they punished for doing things with me? Why does my poppa hate me so much?"

There never would be an answer. No one heard her, and those who did could not answer her. As they did not know the answers either. But over the years she saw the good in them, and she learned to love her family. How she wished they would love her back.

3

They were busy - always working on the farm, or with the machinery, or with animals. Everyone had a job, a purpose, but she had none. "You're too little" they would say. And it would make her very sad, and she would cry.

Every morning she would wake up early, and climb out of her crib. She lifted herself up to the rails, and carefully slid to let herself down. She had to grip the bars hard, so she would not fall. Once out, she would come down the stairs, one step at a time, on her bum, holding onto the rail. She would open the refrigerator door, and take out one of her bottles of milk. Then she would put on her coat, sometimes backwards or upside down. Then put on her brother's cowboy boots that went up over her knees.

At their front door. she would have to stretch as hard as she could on her tippy toes to press the bottom latch to open the door. Then out she would go down the steps, one by one. Careful not to fall. She went on to the road toward the barn. She would walk to the barn in the dark unafraid. Her Momma and her friends were there.

At the barn she was unable to open the door. So she kicked the door repeatedly until someone would open the door for her. Quickly her nickname became Bossy Boots. Her Momma would come and scoop her up, and put her into the calf pen. Her friends were the animals. Once placed inside her half of the calf pen, the calves would try to get her milk bottle. On occasion she shared with the kittens that nestled in the straw beside her. Her Momma scolded her for doing this. But when Momma was not looking, she cuddled her friends near her, and shared her bottle of milk.

The year she turned four, she started showing signs of independence daily. Her two brothers, whom she spent the most time with, were now eleven and twelve years old with varied interests. They learned there was a pigeon group that met near their farm. This lively group had all sorts of prized pigeons. Some were fliers, some were

4

carriers, some were tumblers. Each owner had a different tag on the leg of their pigeon. Often the boys would find those pigeons in the barn searching for food. If they caught them, the owners would pay a good sum of money when returned. So the two boys fashioned crates to put pigeons in, and made a daily round to search for pigeons that showed up at their farm.

One day they decided to go on the barn roof. It was quite easy since the barn roof came almost to the ground on the back side of the barn. One big step and you were on the down slope of the roof. They carried chicken hooks to snag the pigeons by their legs. Then they carried them down the back side of the barn, and put them in a crate. They enlisted April to guard the crate. They were quite busy, and had about eleven pigeons, when some older brothers came along with their mean friends.

"What are you doing?" they asked April, taking away the crate.

"Please don't do that," April asked while reaching up for the crate.

They stood there mocking her, and opened the side door releasing the birds. They laughed at her, pushing her head backwards, and knocking her down to the ground. She sat there, and began to cry. Then she said, "I'm going to tell Momma."

"Oh, you're going to tell your Momma are you?" They carried her up the low end back side of the barn, and placed her in a sitting position on the peak, laughing at her.

April looked at her two brothers on the far end of the roof. "Don't move," they yelled to her. "We will come over."

"You let her sit there," the older boys yelled at April, and they began to throw rocks at her. April ducked the rocks as best as she could, leaning forward each time to avoid the rocks. It was no use, she was being hit, and they hurt her. April lay forward on the roof with her head to the side, and with her hands began scooting, trying to get to where her two brothers were. When all of a sudden, a big rock hit her hands. Then another hit her chest, and she let go. Down, down, down she went, rolling down the steep side of the barn roof. She rolled off of the roof. It was a forty-five foot drop to the ground. She landed on her stomach, and she was stunned. She had fallen a long way, but it only felt like she fell off of the swing. It was not so bad. She did hit her jaw, which bit through her tongue. That hurt, but she just felt stiff.

The group of older boys came running, and they ran down the side bank of the barn. "Is she dead?" one asked in a frightened and excited voice.

April was not about to give them that satisfaction. She pushed her hands into the dirt on the road, forcing her body up, and said, "That did not hurt."

April walked to the house, but it did hurt with every step. April felt shaky inside her body. When she got inside her home, she called to her Momma, and began to cry. Momma had had enough. This was the last straw! Momma come out on the porch, and ordered all of the boys to come in. They did. She told the friends to leave, and to not come back. They were not welcome there anymore. How would they like if their sister was treated like that. "Oh, we don't care," said two. "We don't have a sister," and they laughed.

That day the law was laid down, Momma swore she would call the police if anything else happened to that little girl on this farm or anywhere else.

Throughout the next years, April cherished the days of summer. She was five now, and she loved playing with her two brothers under the big maple tree. They would make roads with their toy trucks and pretend they were working. She would play in the dirt beside them. Sometimes she would go with them fishing in their pond. They would catch Sunfish, Catfish, or some Rainbow Trout for dinner. They took her for rides on their bicycles, balancing her on the front handle bars, telling her to "sit still" or they would fall. They would catching fireflies at night, putting them in a jar. Watching the fireflies light up was fascinating.

They taught her how to catch frogs in the boggy meadow, using flashlights. Often there would be a turtle, and April was told to NEVER pick one up. It might be a snapper who would take her fingers off. So she always called to them to come and see the turtle, which was usually a box turtle of all colors.

They taught her how to set traps to catch raccoons, and they made one of them a pet, calling it Bandit. They would give Bandit sugar cubes, and Bandit would wash the sugar cube in the water. The sugar cube would dissolve, and Bandit would not understand. Then the children laughed.

Once they found a nest of flying squirrels. They took one home, nursed it, and raised it as their pet. It was such fun to see Acorn fly from one door frame to the couch. He loved crackers or anything chewy. Acorn would sit up, and eat beside you, even if he was a little nervous. Soon he would be gone, off on another adventure in the house.

They took April with them deer hunting. She would use branches, one in each hand, and bang them onto trees or the ground to make noise for driving the deer. They also took her small game hunting with the beagle named Nell. April loved to hear Nell bark when she caught scent of a rabbit. Nell was quick. She would use her nose trailing the scent along a wood row or rock wall, and, in no time, she would be driving a rabbit towards her brothers and their single shot, shot guns.

Later that year, in the fall, it was her job to ride their mule, Jumper, to follow the coon dogs. With the lantern tied onto the billet cinch, the mule would trot through fields and woods alike, following the call of the dogs. April sat on the old Army saddle with the split wood in the middle, and hold onto the breast collar because she had to lay down, or she would be knocked off.

She giggled and jostled holding on, sometimes keeping her eyes shut tight. Not that she was afraid, but she did not want a branch poking her eyes. On and on they would go, until they came to where the dogs had the raccoons trapped in a tree, barking all around that tree. She would sit up, and pull on the mules reins. Then take the whistle on a rope around her neck, and blow on it, time after time, so the hunters would know where the dogs were. It was exciting, fast, and sometimes tragic, to see one of their dogs killed by a raccoon's quick movements and sharp claws. In water those dogs did not have a chance.

Oh, those were fun times. Even in cold weather, they would take her sled riding. She loved it outside, and those two brothers were such fun.

She soon got a job of collecting eggs, and taking care of the chickens and ducks. One day, as a hen was nesting on eggs for hatching, she wondered to herself what would happen if a hen's egg was put under a duck that was nesting. And then put that duck egg under the chicken that was nesting. And she did that.

It took twenty-one days for the chicks to hatch, and twenty-eight for the ducklings. In no time the baby duck with the chickens pecked at grass, and scratched with his feet. But he did like to play in water. The chick with the ducks was usually wet. But in time, she learned to swim with them, proving to April that we are products of our environment. No matter who you are, or where you came from, you can change.

Every day April was to make sure the chicken pens were clean, and that they had fresh water and feed. And the ducks too. That was her job daily. The chickens were much more fun to take care of then the dirty ducks. The ducks always pooped liquid, and she had to shake fresh straw for them each and every day.

That year, the fifth year of her life, April was also responsible for giving the calves bottles of milk. One by one she would hold a bottle and steady the calf, and when the calf was done drinking, she put that fed calf on the other side of the pen, and closed the gate. Sometimes there were two or three, other times there may be as many as eleven. April always did her job, and by day three, most of the calves she had trained to drink out of a bucket instead of a bottle. April was very proud that she could teach them so quickly.

Of all the children, April was most suited to work with the animals. It took a lot of patience and care, and the boys were glad to be rid of the job of taking care of the calves. In fact, she did a better job with all the animals than all of the boys. For such a young age, she was very responsible, and cared about all of the animals.

Of all the things they did together, her favorite was the ponies. She would do anything, any chore - wash socks, help them make a bed, pick up garbage, do their chores for them, if they would saddle one of their ponies so she could ride.

In the fall, Momma bought two bay ponies. Baby was to be hers. Bucky was to belong to the boys. He was taller than Baby by a hand (four inches) with a more wild side.

Baby was such a sweet, kind pony. With tiny butterfly kicks, the pony would respond and walk. Anyone could ride her. She reined so easily, and stopped when asked. Bucky, on the other hand, kept true to his name, wild and full of buck and vigor. He would tear off in any direction. Baby was her companion. April would ride her to pick flowers for Momma, or to deliver misdelivered mail to a neighbor.

In time, although she loved Baby, her attention was soon drawn to Bucky. She did not see him as dangerous. He was misunderstood. Often she brought out carrots or apples for the two of them. And Bucky would nicker to her as if to say thank you. April realized that she was the only one truly kind to him.

One day feeling a bit guilty, she gave Baby a little extra hay, and went to Bucky. She decided she would ride him. After watching her brothers saddle him two or three times she was able to saddle up on her own. She brushed him down, put the pad on his back, and he turned his head to watch her. She spoke to him the whole while, "Now Bucky, I am going to take you out riding today, and you're going to be a good boy. Please do not go too fast or scare me, Okay?" and she put her head against his, eye to eye. She felt confident that Bucky did understand her, and that was good enough for her.

All saddled up, she led him outside, and stood on the bucket to reach the stirrup, and climb on. Bucky was so good, he just stood there waiting.

Once on him, she gathered the reins in her hands, and said, "Let's go." He did, a bit faster than Baby, but confidently, and April was not afraid. In time these two would cross creeks, rivers, climb steep hills and rocks and venture into the deep woods. They had many adventures together. Bucky taught April to never be afraid.

Near their farm was a butchering facility. It was well known that they did not follow the laws for disposing of their animal carcasses. They had the habit of driving into a field or woods, and dumping the carcasses. Then they left them there until they rotted away, and became one with the earth. However, that was an attraction to the wild dogs, foxes and coyotes that lived in the wild. April was told to NEVER go up to that area. That area connected to one field of their farm. Being a curious child, she did go there, with Bucky. She would dismount and look around at all of the carcasses. She found many interesting things, which is why she began to say she wanted to be a veterinarian or a doctor when she grew up.

Often on trips to that field, April heard sounds, unlike anything she heard before. She felt that it could be dangerous. She quickly mounted Bucky, and said, "Ha," for him to run. And to hurry as fast as he could go. And he did. As Bucky ran, every once in a while, April could feel his body shift left and then right. She looked under her arm and could see wild dogs chasing them with their teeth exposed. April realized Bucky was kicking at the wild dogs who were chasing them.

Each time Bucky would outrun them, but on several occasions Bucky received bites to his legs. When that happened, April would dab them with Peroxide, and watch it bubble. Then she put an ointment on top, and covered the area with gauze to hold the ointment in place.

On those times, she knew she was going to get a whipping. And dutifully, she stood for her punishment from her Poppa. She knew she was told to stay out, so she would steel her mind to what was to come. When done, she would disappear to the barn. Funny, the pony never held a grudge against her, He never showed the anger that her Poppa did.

It was a short time later that Baby showed signs of failing. She was not sick, but she stopped eating, and did not drink her water. April did all she could, brushing Baby, and talking to her. And Momma called the Vet. Somehow, Baby had contracted shipping fever. It was doubtful she would live. That was THE worst news April had ever heard. She prayed to God to let her pony live.

She promised she would be good, do whatever was asked of her cheerfully, if only he would grant her this small wish. It was not to be. April stayed with Baby all night long, holding the pony's head on her lap. She kept her covered with a comfy blanket, petting her, and talking to her. But by morning, Baby was gone.

April's tears flowed like a stream. Her heart was broken, and she felt guilty because she loved Bucky too. But she never wanted Baby to leave. There was little to console her. She did not want to eat or play. She wanted to be left alone. Then a few days later it was confirmed Bucky, too, had contracted shipping fever. That was too much for her to bear. Surely one pony taken from her was enough.

Maybe God was checking to see if she really cared about this pony. She did. Again she spent days with him, unwilling to leave his side.

In two days, Bucky too was no more. April was sure she wanted to die. She felt like a part of her left. She cried and cried. She would not eat, and there was nothing anyone could do to console her.

Finally her Poppa had enough, and locked her in her room. He did not want to hear one more sniffle. Momma would come up, and ask her to eat some soup, or Jello or pudding. But she refused, and just sat there crying, shaking her head

And this is how it went for four days, until Momma went into April's room, and found her unable to respond. She carried April down stairs, and walked straight out of the house to the garage. She put April on the back seat, and drove her to the hospital.

There April was admitted with dehydration. IV's were in her arms, and she remained in the hospital for several days. Momma stayed with her. She had to explain to the nurse about all of the black and blue marks, the history of fractures, and the scars from burn marks.

The social workers came one day, and tried to encourage Momma to leave. The history of April and the hospital was beginning to be routine. It was not fair to the child. If this kept up, they would recommend that an agency step in, and take April away for adoption.

Momma was beside herself. How could she get them to let her alone? Why? Why were they like this to her? She was so young and innocent. What joy did they get out of hurting her like this?

Momma knew she could not leave Poppa. She felt trapped. Having had Tuberculosis, she knew she would never be allowed to work in a pubic job - not ever. So how would she be able to earn an income in order to raise April, and also take care of them both? It was impossible! She would just have to be more careful, and watch April more closely.

April learned that animals were truly her friends. They had a bird dog Poppa used for pheasant hunting. She was a speckled bird dog named Candy, and had bonded with April as a puppy. April learned that if she were close enough to get into Candy's dog house, then no one could get to her. The dog would bark, and lunge at whoever was trying to get April. Yes, the dog house had spider webs, it was dusty, and had bones, but April felt safe there. And that was the best feeling in the world.

The big horses April was not allowed to be near. "She will get kicked or stepped on," Poppa said. But that was so far from the truth. If one of the older boys was chasing her in the barn, and if she could duck under the stall gate, she knew she was safe.

All she had to do is stand under the horse, and the horse would protect her. It did not matter if it was the mare or the stallion. Either one would go after the boys with their teeth baring, and rearing to strike them. After they were gone, April would come out, and thank them. She patted them on their faces, they would hang their heads low, and seemed to understand. When the pathway was clear, April would make a B-line to the house or to the barn to find her Momma.

It was true April had suffered at the hands of her brothers. Sometimes it was hard to tell who hurt her the most. Poppa did, not so much with his hands, but with his words. Poppa was negligent at helping to stop the boys from hurting April. And this had to stop, it just had to.

That spring, as usual, the boys were instructed to take all of the junk out of the double corn crib. As the corn was shelled, and used, the bin became empty. Trash, such as a board that broke, or a broken chair, was put in the empty side of the bin. By spring they had accumulated barrels, cardboard, and all sorts of burnable things to build a bonfire. Piece by piece was brought out. And soon they had a pile that stood thirty feet high.

A piece of newspaper was used, and "whoosh", the pile caught fire, and soon the fire was really going. And did it burn. It burned for almost a week. Finally after 6 days, the fire was down to dark embers, but still hot. The older boys were out at the fire jumping over the hot ashes.

When they saw April coming along with the basket of eggs she had collected from the laying hens, their friends ran to get her. They grabbed her holding her close to the fire, and she could feel the heat on her face. "Jump it" they yelled, shoving her a little too close. "Jump over the fire."

"I can't," she said. "I will fall."

"No you won't," said one. "It's easy, watch me," and he ran, jumping over the fire with ease.

"I don't think so," April said. "I'm supposed to put the eggs away because Momma wants some to make dessert for supper."

"Oh, pooh. You can do that later." And again, she felt hands at her back pushing her. "Come on, jump it. We want to see you jump it."

There was no way out. April backed away, setting the egg basket down. If she tried to run, there would be no telling what they would do to her this time. She stood back and ran, lifting her legs wide to jump the fire. As she did a wire caught on her feet, and brought her right down into the center of those burning ashes. She was stunned, everyone was.

As quickly as she could, she got up and ran. She ran to the back of the house to hide. She was afraid. Afraid Poppa would hit her for jumping into the fire. Afraid of what the boys would do to her because she failed to jump over the embers. She sat there hunched down, she heard some of the boys coming to the back of the house.

"There she is," one said. "Quick go in and get Momma." There was a fast scurry of feet, and they were gone.

In seconds Momma was there. "What happened, sweetie? Oh, momma, I fell in the fire." She went to lift April, but her arms were stuck on her legs. April's skin had melted together.

"Help me," she said to the older boys. The four boys helped Momma lift April up, and took her into the house.

"Go to the bathroom," Momma said. And standing her up in the bathtub, Momma began to wipe her skin, ashes, wood, and metal pieces from her body. As Momma wiped, the skin began to weep and burst open. There was a lot of blood, and she wiped April all over - over and over. Momma wiped her until her body was clean, then placed April's body on the day bed in the parlor room on top of a clean white sheet.

Next, Momma ordered the boys to bring her the box of petroleum jelly she had just purchased, the case of it. And she began to soothe the petroleum jelly all over April's burned body. April did not remember, or know. The pain was too great. She went in and out of sleep. The family doctor came to the farm, and said Momma had saved April's life. He left a glass straw for April to drink her food, as her lips were full of burn blisters.

April stayed on that day bed for months. Slowly she began to show signs of improvement. Her hair began to grow back, and her blisters disappeared. Only one huge blister remained on the abdomen. It was long from the impression of a hot metal rod she must have fallen on.

Her two brothers, Tim and John doted on her. They would get anything she wanted from the refrigerator or cupboard. They would read to her, talk to her, sing to her, and within minutes April would be asleep.

Momma moved a small television into the parlor room. Adjusting the antenna, the two of them would watch cartoons, Daniel Boone, or Disney movies.

The doctor came to see April's progress every week. He talked to Momma about the "problem" of all the accidents that had happened to April.

"She is only six years old, and her patient file is thicker than yours. And you had TB," he said.

Momma looked at him with tears welling in her eyes. She did not know what to do. She said, "She is in kindergarten now, and in time, as years go by, she will be older and able to take care of herself.

The Dr. relied, "If she makes it." April did heal, without one scar, physically.

Later, when April was up and about, she wanted to go outside. She loved to ride her bicycle. She was now back in school, and her hair had grown back almost to shoulder length. Their driveway was dirt and now muddy from the rain that had fallen for days.

The township was working on the road, tar and chipping it, so no one was allowed to drive on it. They were planning to black top it after the weather dried out. For now there were tiny sharp stones all over the road until the blacktop could be finished. Since no cars were on the road, they had to walk 2½ miles to their school bus stop. But on the plus side, now you could ride your bicycle on the road with no cars to worry about. The mud flew up onto her legs and pants, but she did not care. It was fun.

Later, after chores and supper, April was in the bathtub washing. All of a sudden the door flew open, and it was Momma. "Quick April, go as fast as you can to the end of the road, and open it. The ambulance is on its way, and the road blocks will not allow them through. You need to open the road. Go as fast as you can. Poppa is in trouble."

And she did. She put on her underwear and t-shirt as fast as she could. She went out the door, and began to run - no socks, no shoes, she just ran. She noticed her dog was were running beside her, and she was thankful. It was a long way to go. She ran and ran and ran. Her feet began to

16

bleed from the sharp chip stones. As much as she tried to stay out of them, it was impossible. She ran with her head down to watch, but she had to keep going. On and on she went until at last she came up the little hill, and saw the road blocks. They were huge white saw horses with big round yellow lights on the top. With a huge push, one fell over. As it fell over, in rushed the ambulance. It rushed past April to get to her house as fast as they could.

April sat down along the side of the bank to look at her feet. They were cut, but not deep. But they did hurt. She walked hobbling all the way home. When she got there, the house was empty, so she crawled back into the tub to wash and clean her feet. She stepped out on a towel, and there was no blood. She breathed a sigh of relief.

April went into the stairwell, and sat there. She was afraid. She did not know what had happened. How bad was it? Why was she alone? What would happen to her? So she sat there, and waited and prayed.

There was another storm looming. The lightening cracked, and thunder boomed. April jumped each time.

In time they all came home, except Poppa. He had a heart attack, and would not be home for several days or maybe even weeks depending on the damage to his heart. That is what John told her. So now April knew she would have some leeway, but would have to stick close by Momma as always.

And then, all too soon, Poppa was home. as grouchy as ever, and now he was limited as to what he could do, physically.

It was now fall, and her world began to change. The older boys continued to taunt her, and pick on her for no reason. And Momma was not always nearby. That year her Poppa decided it would be a good idea for the boys to quit school early and help more at the farm. Momma was dead set against that idea.

"What if framing is not what they want to do?" she said.

"I don't care what they want. There is too much work for one man to do, and they will learn more here on the farm than in school," was Poppa's reply. Momma knew this would not be the last of it, and the boys would not want to leave school. She knew each had a chosen plan for themselves.

Whether it was the Army, the Navy, or to go to college, she knew they would be home more. They would be unhappy, and April would be their target. For now she would bide her time. It was still late fall and Poppa would not make the boys quit school. Poppa would have to prepare them in the late spring and summer.

As next spring came around it was her 6th year, and time seemed to drag. Things at home became worse. There was constant arguing and fighting. It was not uncommon for April to find a reclusive spot where she could not be found.

One such place was upstairs in the window sills. Those window ledges were very deep and wide. It was easy for her to slip behind the curtain, and sit there reading a book, or just being quiet for safety's sake. She became an easy target for bullying. It seemed her brothers took out their frustrations with their Poppa on her.

One afternoon as she sat in the window sill of her bedroom, she heard the older boys and their friends. They were looking for her everywhere. She held her breath, and did not move, not an inch. They looked in each room.

"She's not in here. She's not in here either." They looked and looked. There were girls with them too, older girls. They must have been in high school. April did not know them.

As they each went into a bedroom with a girl, April heard noises unlike anything she ever heard before. And she became afraid. She hopped down ever so quietly from the window sill, and began to creep down the hallway to the stairs. When a board creaked, a door flew open, and there stood one of the older boys' friends.

"I found her," and he grabbed her by the arm. April tried to get away, but he was much bigger and stronger than she was.

"Please let me go," she begged him over and over.

"What?" he said to someone in the room. "Me do her? Are you kidding?"

Do her? What did that mean, do her? Oh, April was so afraid that her heart was thumping, and she tried over and over to get away. She slipped on the floor trying to wriggle away from him, when he reached over and picked her up. He put her on his shoulder, and went into a bedroom, throwing her on the bed.

He pulled down her pants and panties, pulling them down all the way to her ankles. She kept trying to get away, screaming. He slapped her in the mouth saying, "Shut up." He shoved her down onto the bed, spreading her legs as far as he could. Then he laid on her, holding her arms above her head. She felt a sharp piercing pain inside her, and began to scream and cry. With his face, he hit her, and said, "Shut up, or I am really going to hurt you. Stay still."

"I won't, I won't stay still. Get off of me, and you're hurting me. She thrashed left to right, never staying still, trying to get him off of her. With one hand he pinned her arms, and with the other hand below he tried to push something inside her.

This time April leaned forward in almost a sitting position. She opened her mouth, and bit his nose clamping down with her teeth so hard that he let her go. "Jesus God, that hurt," he yelled holding his bloody nose and pushing her away. April ran downstairs as fast as she could.

Momma was not there, so she ran outside to the barn. Momma was not there either, so she hid in the stables by the stallion. She stayed there all day crying, holding onto the stallions legs for support. She hurt. Whatever he did to her, hurt her. There was blood on her thighs. She was hurt, and she was mad. So angry that she wanted to kill him.

Being thugs as they were, they came looking for her. She heard them talk about getting in trouble, but April did not move. Neither did the stallion, he just stood there munching hay like he was all alone.

Milking time she was still there. She knew her Momma would be in the barn. She knew she had her jobs to do, but she couldn't. She just couldn't.

April left the stallion, petting his nose. She peeked out to see if the coast was clear. She walked to the other side of the barn. She knew she had chores to do. As she passed through an alleyway, she quickly past two of her brothers. One saw her, and he tried to grab her. She ran to her Momma and told her what had happened.

Right then all of the milker's were taken off of the cows, and Momma had a whip in her hand. She approached the older boys asking questions, and lashing at them. They were not laughing now. They tried to get out, but John had locked the door from the outside, securing the latch. Momma went to the telephone in the barn, and called the police. They came, and asked April to show them what had happened.

With her Momma at her side holding on to her, April did show them. She was brave, only later she sobbed into her mother's dress. She was hurt and ashamed.

The policeman was disgusted. He swore and spit. He questioned the boys, and finally they gave up the other boy's name. That older boy never came to their farm again, not ever. Her brothers were not happy with her. They told her that she could have hurt herself riding a bike. April spit on them.

April was convinced they were not her brothers. They were evil beings in her home, and never would she go near them, not ever again. People who love you do not hurt you, or treat you badly.

Dinnertime became a dreaded time. She often had her face pushed into her food because she was not eating. She instinctively knew not to cry. She had to sit there, and endure. Often she would slide out of her chair and sit on the floor. She would eat the food that had fallen on the floor. It was better than sitting at the table.

Once again the older boys were bored and looking for fun. They caught and tied April with car chains inside the garage door. They held her up, and chained her to the door. It was well past seven o'clock when Momma noticed April was missing. At the mention of this, two older boys got up, and went outside to get her. They found April dirty and tired. She came in crying, but one look from Poppa, and she stopped crying. She took in a deep breath, and headed upstairs. Momma came up, and held her, rocking her, and telling her it would be alright.

She gave April a bath, put on her pajamas, and gave her a small amount of dinner. Of course Momma worried, but how could she stop the bullying of her little girl when her Poppa did it. And that encouraged the boys. Sighing, she went downstairs to find the conversation full of laughter at the "good joke" the boys had played on April.

Mother was furious. "Joke? You call this a joke? How would you like it if you were tied up somewhere unable to get free, with nothing to eat or drink?"

The one son answered, "No one is big enough to do that to me," and he laughed.

"Oh, really?" Momma said. "We will see. We will see." As she began to clear the table setting, all eyes were on Momma. She was never cross, never angry. But just like when April ratted out their friend, and they got whipped, Momma looked that angry. That look on her face said she was way more than a little cross.

That evening she was determined to speak to her husband about the boys' behavior to her husband. "This bullying, this hurting, MUST STOP," Momma said.

"So what," he said. "It's good for her to be treated a little badly. She needs to get used to it. That will prepare her for life." Momma began to realize what he was saying.

"So," Momma said. "You believe it is okay for someone, anyone, to pick on your daughter, and treat her badly. So often that she has a chart thicker than anyone in this family?"

Poppa answered, "I don't care what happens to her. I wouldn't care if gypsies stole her, or if she just disappeared. In fact, I'd consider it a good thing." And that was that.

Two of the youngest boys heard that conversation, on their way out of the bathroom. They were not supposed to have heard it, but they did. And the two youngest boys sat up, awake on their beds, trying to decide what to do. A plan was hatched.

"She is never going to make it," Tim said.

"I know," replied John. "But what can we do?"

"We can find money, and send her far away, so she will be safe,"said Tim.

"We will be in a lot of trouble," said John.

"No we will not, no one will know. We will make it seem like an accident. She will just disappear, but we will need to make a plan," said Tim. And so a plan was hatched, developed and planned out for the safety of their little sister. They knew they would miss her, and wonder about her. But this was to ensure their little sister would live.

It was decided they would raid the money jar kept in the top-most cupboard, saved for emergencies. Then there was Poppa's wallet. It had a secret compartment that they saw once when they were all in the hardware store. Their eyes almost popped out when they saw one hundred dollar bills stuffed inside the tiny compartment. And Poppa had a secret shelf under the dresser. It had envelopes with a lot of money. Momma also kept money in a drawer, not a lot, but all together, it would surely be enough to send their sister to a safe place. And they had money in their metal banks. It would take time to use a knife to get the coins to fall out of the slit on the bottom.

It was not often that their family would go to town together, being a big family they usually had to take two vehicles. And it was decided that they would all go together to shop for new white Easter shirts and ties, and maybe some shoes.

The boys worked secretly, taking April's favorite stuffed tiger and making a slit in the top. They put a sock with money inside and sewed it back together. One item at a time - they rolled her clothing, underwear, socks, pants, shorts, shirts, two dresses, pajamas, a tooth brush, a brush for her hair, some hair bands, and many other things. Most were rolled tightly and put into small ziplock bags. These things were kept secretly hidden in their drawers, or under their bed.

They had time, but worked feverishly. They squirreled away things they thought she would use, eat, or want, including her treasured paper, pencils, crayons, and tissues. All were in her small blue suitcase that she took with her everywhere. They even stole some family pictures and some of their school photos.

So on that afternoon, they took the backpack with them containing April's clothing and needed items and her blue suitcase. They brought her tiger that she loved. And last minute, while everyone was dressing or showering, they went in different directions to get the money they decided on weeks ago. Once done, they all piled into the cars. They made sure April sat between them, holding onto her tiger. The backpack was on the floor of the driver's side at Tim's feet, and April never ever went anywhere without her blue suitcase.

It had begun to rain lightly, but Momma had to turn on the wipers. And they made a funny sound. At their destination at the store in town, Momma parked the car.

She told them to stay together, and not to separate in the store. Poppa had arrived earlier, and was parked further down near the store's back entry. He had taken 4 of the older boys with him.

As Momma and the other five children headed into the store, all but Tim, John and April. The two boys took April's hand, one on each side of her. They were the last to enter the store. But before they entered, they let the doors close in front of them. They turned around, and crossed the street to the bus station. They pulled the door open, and stepped inside.

The only one present was a temporary clerk. The boys had never seen this man before, and he obviously did not like children. "What do you want in here?" he said.

Tim spoke, "Our sister is going to our Aunt's home in California. How much is a ticket?"

"What part of California?" the man snapped.

"Fresno," Tim said.

The clerk looked at his map, and did some calculating on his sheet. "That will be eighty-four dollars," the man said. Tim pulled out four twenty dollar bills and four ones. The man watched him carefully.

"Where are your parents?" he said.

"Over there. They are buying some last minute things and something for our Aunt," said John.

The clerk looked up through the thick lenses of his glasses. He saw a woman wave. She was wearing a long brown dress coat. However, she was waving to her husband, as if to say, I am here, as he pulled his car into his parking spot. The boys recognized her. She was the lady who worked at the gas department. She sat at the window, and would smile at them as they walked to school. The bus clerk thought this was the children's mother waving. She was there, so it seemed alright to him. The clerk went on, and clipped out a ticket. As he finished, a bus pulled up.

He handed the ticket over the counter, and the boys pulled April aside and said, "You are going on a nice trip. Your things are here," as one put the backpack on her back. Here is your sweater if you get cold, and there is a secret place in your tiger with money when you need it. Your suitcase has some pictures in the back behind the mirror, so you don't forget us. She looked at them quizzically, not fully understanding.

"Aren't you coming too?" she asked.

The boys looked at each other, and John quickly said, "No we can't. We have too much work to do, but you can go. You are going to have so much fun, and meet so many nice people. And then you will be back in no time."

As the bus driver tapped on the window motioning with his hands to board, the boys quickly gave her a hug and a kiss on her forehead and cheek. Tim had to turn away to hide his tears. "Now you go, and remember to be good, and don't you cry. Be brave and have fun! Okay? They hugged her one last time, "Okay, you better go."

They exited the door while holding her hand to help her up the first step of the bus, and handed the bus driver her ticket. They let go of her hand, and the bus driver took it helping her into the seat behind his.

There April sat with her tiger on her lap, the backpack on the floor beside her feet, and her small blue suitcase beside her on the window side. As the door closed, she looked and saw her brothers across the street, standing in the rain that had begun to come down harder.

The windows of the bus were streaked with rain drops sliding down the windows. The boys never left that spot. They stayed as the bus started, and began to drive away. They waved, and stayed there in that spot until the bus was out of sight. April waved back, and then settled in on her seat, just watching and hearing the noise on the bus. Soon the bus engine started, and began to pull away from the curb onto its next destination. It seemed like a long time. She began to get sleepy, and soon was asleep. The bus went on and on and on . . .

The boys quickly went to the store, opened the door, and went inside. They headed downstairs to the bathroom, wiping their heads and clothes with paper towels. They stayed down in the bottom of the store basement area that was the toy section of the store. They felt as long as they stayed there, their sister had a better chance to get away. They soon were lost in the boxes and items on the store shelves. They looked at toys they had never seen or heard of. While one of them was always watching for the others to come and find them.

It was about forty-five minutes later when one of their brothers came down and found them. Then another came, and soon six boys were there looking. Some of them taking an item to purchase. A lady clerk came downstairs so she could ring up the purchases. She put their items in a bag, and stapled the top with the receipt attached.

Before long the older boys called from the stairs of the store for everyone to come together, to go back upstairs. Once there, Momma and Poppa were at a checkout, and soon they all exited the store. Everyone had bags, some 4 or five of them. The bags were put in the trunks and some in the back seats. It was a bit chaotic. They did not notice April was gone, and the two did not say a word.

On the way home, Momma looked in the rearview mirror, and four or five of them were all piled up sleeping. Bags were piled all around, some on the floor, some on the seat, some bags on top of them, and she smiled.

Once home, they all headed inside leaving the bags in the car. It was late, and they were all tired. Nothing would spoil in the bags, so they could bring them all in after morning chores. The two boys went in, and hurried to put a pillow under the covers to fool everyone into thinking April had crawled under her covers, and was in bed sleeping. And it worked.

No one suspected a thing, and as the night went on, the two boys looked at each other across from their beds. Tim said, "I hope she is far, far away so they cannot find her, and make her come back."

"I know," said John. Who added, "Remember, we do not know a thing!"

The next morning at breakfast is when the calamity began. It was sheer panick. Everyone looked for April. Momma had to wait to call the store, because it was too early. Who was April with? Everyone shrugged. They thought she was with someone else in the family, but did not know who. Poppa was the only one who was silent. He sat in his easy chair reading the paper, as if he was not concerned at all. In fact, he felt gleeful inside, a relief.

Momma was crying. Some of the boys had a look of terror in their eyes. Where was April? What had happened to her? On that Saturday everyone looked and looked, people were called and questions were asked. There were no answers, no one could answer their questions. Two could, but for the sake of their sister, they both kept looking for her, just like everyone else. They too cried and said nothing.

The police were called. The hospital was called. No one, no one saw her. How could a six-year-old little girl just disappear? It was then that the social workers came out to the house, and began to ask Poppa and Momma about the history of "accidents" their daughter had. Poppa was not bothered. He said he did not know. He said that the child was careless.

Momma could not take any more. She pulled the social worker into the parlor room, sat down, and began to tell of the seven years of abuse. As she sobbed, she tried to explain she did not know where to go for help. The case worker closed her book, and said, "Well now you will not need to look for help. It seems as though this situation has taken care of itself.

"What do you mean?" Momma asked.

The case worker replied, "This child is far better off away from here. I do not know any more than you do about where this child is or what happened to her, good or bad. But I can honestly tell you, that since you are unable to help her, she is better off wherever she is. Nothing against you, but this situation is far too bad for a little girl to handle on her own. She has too much stacked up against her."

The case worker got up, spoke to the police, and they all left. And that is how April escaped from a life of abuse, with the aid of the two who did care about her, but were voiceless. And April never forgot them. Not ever.

Leaving Home

It seemed like every few minutes April awoke to noises. People were coming on the bus. She strained her eyes, and saw a sign. But being unable to read, she asked the bus driver, what the sign said. "New Jersey," he replied.

"Do I get off of the bus now?" asked April.

"Oh, no," he said. "You will be on this bus with me for quite a while yet."

April was happy. She was so uncertain of where she was going, but the bus driver was nice, and most of the people coming on the bus kept to themselves. And as the bus began to pull out, most of the passengers were sleeping. She could tell by their snoring, just like Poppa did.

During the ride, being curious, April asked the bus driver questions. He did not seem to mind. He was not a very tall man. He had a big belly, but he was not fat. He had brown hair with silver and grey. He also had a small beard, and wore glasses. He had a nice voice, the kind that is calm and easygoing. He never got excited or said swear words when driving. He sometimes called other drivers "crazies".

His name was Ed. He was married to the most beautiful woman in the world, and they had three daughters, Joan, Becky and Donna, all grown and gone on their own. They had one grandson that he did not see much because his daughter married a military guy, and they moved around a lot. They were living in Hawaii since last year. The other two daughters did not have children, and he was hoping they would settle down soon with good men who would make good fathers. April was still young, but she understood that all too well.

Ed said, "But for now, it is my sweetheart and I, and we fill out our days working all week. We like to go to visit friends on the weekends and have dinner out. We love to travel to the countryside."

"My wife thinks she is a photographer of sorts. I bought her a really nice camera two years ago, and she loves to take pictures, lots of them. I don't mind, but I don't like to travel too far. I do that for a living, driving bus," and then he smiled. "I like children, and hope to have a lot of grandchildren. So little girl, you sure came on the right bus. I promise to keep my eye out for you, and take good care of you. All I ask is that you be a good girl, and listen when I tell you something. Okay?"

April nodded her head, and said, "I will."

It was late, way past her bed time, and she hugged her tiger close. She felt the warm air coming from the heater beside the bus driver. He looked at her in the mirror and asked, "Are you too hot or are you cold?"

"Oh, no," she said. "I am just right." The bus driver smiled at her, and then kept his eyes on the road.

In that mirror if she leaned forward, April could see many of the people on the bus. There were black people, people with slanted eyes, and some who looked like they were rich, in their fine dressed up clothing. She had never seen such folks before. But soon, she began to get sleepy, and leaned against the seat and slept.

That is how the bus trip went - people got on, and people got off. April wondered when she could go to the bathroom. She stood and asked the bus driver. "Oh, we will be stopping in about ten minutes if you can wait, but there is a bathroom in the back of the bus."

So THAT is where that funny smell came from. She squinted her nose, and said, "I'll wait."

"Good idea," the bus driver said, smiling at her.

True to the bus driver's word, they did pull into a restaurant in less than 10 minutes. April watched the little hand on the bus driver's big watch on his left wrist. It was easy to see, and gave her something to do.

At that stop, April tugged at the bus driver's sleeve. "Is this where I get off to go to the bathroom?" she asked.

"Yes. Yes it is," he replied. And as an older woman with a fur coat came towards the exit, he asked her, "Ma'am, if you are going to the ladies room? Would you mind tending to this little girl? She has to go, if you know what I mean."

"Oh, yes. I am," the woman said. "I don't mind taking her along at all, come along now. What is your name?" she asked.

"April, my name is April, and I must pee." And the woman laughed.

The woman was older, about forty. At least that seemed old to April. She was a pretty lady, with greying hair that she wore short, like a pageboy haircut. She put her hair behind her ears a lot. She wore some makeup, to make her cheeks rosy red. And she wore a lot of jewelry - rings on most of her fingers, and necklaces, about three of them. One was a magnifying glass.

The woman had on a big tan sweater with big buttons and fur around the neck. She had on pants that were black and fancy. But April sensed much more about this woman, and her gut instincts told her this woman was kind and full of love. April liked her right away.

They found the restroom just in time. April almost put her hands between her legs to stop from going, but as they went into the restroom, someone came out of a stall, she ran in, and pulled her panties down as she walked. "Well, someone had to go bad," someone said. The woman with her, held the stall door closed for privacy. And then when April came out, the woman told April to go wash her hands, and wait for her.

April watched others as they put their hands under a round-shaped ball. Then they would push up with their hands, and soap came out. She had never seen soap like that before. And when it was her turn, she was amazed at how soft the soap was compared to the bar soap they used at home. And this soap smelled nice too.

She finished washing her hands, and went to find a towel. There was a heater on the wall that people pushed on a big silver button, and hot air would come whooshing out. She was so amazed at that drier. People came and pushed that button, she thought that was the greatest thing ever. Sure would be great to dry your hair, or warm a chicken pen with. As the woman she was with came to her, she asked April, "Did you dry your hands?"

"No Ma'am," April replied. "I did not."

"Well," the woman said, "let's get it done." They did together, and that was fun. April giggled, which made the woman begin to laugh too.

When they came out, the woman said, "My name is Barbara. April, Are you hungry?" Now April had been taught to say "no" when asked if she wanted something from strangers. But her stomach was growling, and she did not know what to do. Finally she looked up at the kind woman and told her.

"Oh, my goodness. You do not need to be afraid of me. I have eleven grandchildren, and they ask me for things all of the time. How about you pretend I am your Grandma, and you can ask me for anything. Okay?" said Barbara.

"Okay," April said and they entered into the restaurant.

What a place! April had never seen anything like this. Table after table with people sitting at it, each having a different meal on their plates. She wondered who the cook was to be able to cook so many different dinners in such a short time. They sat at the table the hostess brought them to. April sat down, and reached up to put a napkin on her lap. "Well, isn't that nice," said Barbara, "I can tell your Momma taught you good manners."

"Yes, Ma'am. She did," said April.

Soon a young girl came over with long brown braided hair. April thought she was very pretty. "Hello, my name is Sarah. I will be your waitress. Do you know what you want, or do you want to take some time?"

"Oh, we just sat down," said Barbara. "We will need a little time."

Barbara looked at April, and said, "April, pick something you like and get it. We don't want to spend a lot of time here. We need to get back on that bus."

April looked at Barbara, and tears began to well in her eyes, "I don't have any money to buy food," she said.

"Oh, come on now," Barbara said, reaching for her napkin to wipe April's tears. "I thought we were pretending that I was your Grandma, and I as buying your breakfast?"

April took a big breath that was more like a shudder sigh, and said, "Alright."

Soon a plate of home fries, scrambled eggs and two pieces of bacon were placed before April. She quickly put the bacon in a napkin, and rolled it up. Barbara watched her, but said nothing. April and her companion ate their breakfasts and made small talk. "Where are you traveling to?" Barbara asked.

"To my Aunt's home far away," April answered.

"Do you know where she lives?" Barbara asked.

"I am not sure of the town name, it's in California," April said smiling.

"You are a brave little girl going all that way by yourself. Is your mother sick that she did not come with you?" Barbara asked.

April began to swing her legs under the table. She did that when she was a little scared, or did not know what to say. "Yes, my Momma had TB for a long time," answered April. Barbara just stared. My word, this little girl and her family must be having a terrible hardship. In her mind she wondered how she could help.

Barbara said, "April, you do not have money to buy food here? Did your family send you on this trip without money?" Barbara asked.

April was unsure what to say, then answered. "I have some money, but not enough to eat in places like this. I can buy hotdogs, or ice cream cones, but not fancy food in restaurants," she said.

Barbara coughed at April's answer, almost losing her mouthful of food. Her family must be awfully backwards, which was difficult to believe considering how well disciplined and what good manners this little girl had. "Well, each to their own ways," she said to herself.

Some of the patrons from the bus began to move to the counter to pay for their food. And Barbara said, "We must finish our breakfast soon, or we will not be able to get on the bus in time." They both began gulping down their food, finishing with Barbara's tea and April's milk. Soon they were at the counter paying for their breakfast. That took Barbara some time since she was getting some other things. Then they exited the restaurant, and she held April's hand so she would board the bus. Barbara stayed outside talking to people. She went from one to another.

The bus driver came on the bus, and asked April, "Are you full? Did you eat well?"

"Yes," April replied smiling, "I did. Thank you."

Soon the passengers all began to board the bus. Barbara was one of the last, as she boarded she handed April a white paper bag. "Here are some goodies for your trip," and she quickly turned to the bus driver, and said, "I collected some money for our little passenger. If she needs to eat, take it out of this. I collected it for her."

"Oh, I understand," said the bus driver, and he promptly reached for his billfold in his back pocket, and put in fifteen dollars. "I promise to take good care of her on my leg of the trip."

"Thank you for your integrity and honesty," Barbara said. And she reached over to him and hugged him. Then as she went to the back of the bus, she stopped and touched April's nose.

The bus driver looked at April, and said, "I will look after you until we reach Tennessee, then you will have another driver. I hope he is a good man, but only time will tell." And soon the bus engine started, and they were on their way.

April looked at some of her books, and drew some pictures on the paper in her suitcase. A very large black man came up, and sat in back of her. "Whatcha drawing?" he asked.

"Oh, not so much," April said. "Here, you want to draw some?" and she handed back two sheets of paper and a pencil.

"Naw I ain't good at drawing and such things like that. I play football. I am going to college to play football. Have you ever heard of UCLA? It is a college in California, and I hear you are going to California, too." April shook her head, she was not sure what college was. She thought someone in the family went to a school to become an electrician, but she was not sure if that was college or not.

"Do you know football?" he asked.

April shook her head no, and asked, "Will you teach me?" The man laughed and took her paper and drew lines, with stick people he tried explaining offense, and defense, and yard lines.

April liked this man immediately. He was kind to her, and took time with her to explain something when she did not understand. April thought that someday this man would be a good Poppa. After about an hour, April yawned and the man said, "Okay, I am getting sleepy too. I better go back to my seat, so you get some sleep."

April asked him, "Will you give me a hug for a nap?" The man laughed a big laugh.

"Sure I will," and he did. He partially picked April up squeezing her gently to his chest, and kissed her cheek. April hugged her arms around his neck snuggling to him. Oh, if only her Poppa had been like this. Then the man left to go back to his seat on the bus. April curled up on her seat using her tiger as a pillow. And the bus engine and familiar sounds on the bus soon had her fast asleep.

Again the bus stopped, but April did not wake, not through the lunch or boarding. Many people looked at her sleeping, and made comments like, "Look at that Angel," "Look at her sleeping like a little lamb." Some just smiled, and went on their way. April was not fully aware. She was in and out of sleep, and did not wake up until the day began to turn to dusk.

When she awoke, some people on the bus were listening to things in their ears, some were reading, some were watching a movie on the bus TV.

April had the urge to go. She knew that sooner or later she and that bathroom were destined to meet. And the time was now. She put her feet on the floor, and slowly began walking, holding onto the round metal bars on each seat. The walk was quite jerky because of the driving.

She stopped at the back of the bus, and she could see the bathroom, but she could smell it first. April took a big breath holding it in, opened the door and closed it behind her. Inside it was not so bad. There was a strong smell of Pine Sol and ammonia. Momma used to use Pine Sol to clean, and she put ammonia on garbage bags so the animals would not tear them open. April went to the bathroom, but there was no place to wash her hands. She came out, and, as she walked, there was a piece of wet towel dangling in the aisle in front of her. It was to wash her hands, and the person holding it was Barbara. April said, "Thank you," and almost skipped to her seat.

Her brothers, Tim and John, were right. The people were nice, and it was fun. No one was mean to her. She could do pretty much what she wanted to do, and no one complained.

On and on the bus went. They crossed many states, April began to keep track. From New Jersey they went on through Delaware and their next stop was Maryland . . .

At the stop in Maryland, April sat in her seat as the people began to exit the bus. The bus driver patted April's hand, and asked, "Are you getting off?"

"Yes, as soon as Barbara comes off," April answered. As Barbara came down the bus aisle, she stopped and smiled at April.

"Will you come join me for dinner?" She asked.

"Yes," and April jumped up, and hugged her.

They saw a place to eat that Barbara was familiar with and she asked April, "Do you like seafood, April?"

"Oh, yes I do. I love fish, fish sticks," she answered.

Barbara laughed. "Okay, let's go" she said. They had to cross over a plank of wood to enter the Sailor's Delight. As they crossed to the restaurant, April saw fish in the water below. They were so colorful, orange, yellow and white. She wanted a closer look, but Barbara pulled her along.

Once inside, April stepped on something slippery on the floor. They were peanut hulls. She picked up a piece, and asked Barbara, "Why do people throw this on the floor?"

Barbara laughed, and answered her, "They throw them on the floor to polish the wooden floors." April was astounded, never in her life would she ever believe this. It was like throwing garbage on the floor. She tossed the piece she had onto the floor, and went with Barbara who a server was leading to a table. Barbara looked at April and said, "Now April, I would like you to try something. I need you to trust me to order food for you. I would like you to try eating something you have never had before. I believe you will like it."

"Oh, okay," April said.

Barbara spoke with the waitress, and in no time at all their meals arrived at their table. Barbara had a huge shelled thing on her plate. Barbara could see April staring, and she told her, "April, this is a lobster, would you like to taste it?"

"Yes, I think I would," she replied. Barbara took her fork, and pulled a piece of lobster meat out of the lobster. She held it in the air towards April. April took the piece into her mouth, and tasted it as she chewed. "I like that. I really like lobster."

Barbara beamed and smiled, "I just knew you would." April had on her plate some things she had never seen. Some were squiggly, like in a question mark, and all colored pink. She picked one up, and Barbara said, "That is shrimp." and April put it in her mouth tasting and chewing. The shrimp was a bit chewy, not like the lobster at all, but she liked shrimp. Next there were white quarter-sized things. "Those are scallops," Barbara said. April popped one in her mouth, tasting and chewing. That scallop was softer to chew then the shrimp. Then there were brown, round-like things, but puffy. "Try that," Barbara encouraged her. April cut a piece in half, and saw it was pink inside. She put it in her mouth, tasting and chewing. And she loved it. Barbara saw April's eyes get wide, and quickly April put the other half in as well. "Those are crab patties. I was not sure if you'd like them."

"Oh, I do," said April.

The two ate and enjoyed their meal. They were so full, they couldn't have dessert. "Oh, I am so full," said Barbara.

And April said, "Stuffed." Barbara laughed.

"Oh, I so enjoy your company little one. You are so delightful to be around. I wish you could meet my grandchildren. You could teach them a few things, like manners. April just smiled at her.

"I like you too, Miss Barbara," April said. "I hope my Aunt in California is just like you."

"Awe, you're so sweet," replied Barbara. "Okay, if we can waddle to the checkout counter, we will go," she said. They scooted out of their seats to pay for their meals. Barbara handed April some money, and asked, "April would you please put this money on the table for the waitress's tip?"

"Okay," said April. And she did, she took the handful of bills and coins, and placed them in the center of the table, and came skipping back. April did not know this, but this was a test. Barbara wanted to see if, even poor, April was honest, or if she would pocket the money. But she did as asked. She was honest. Barbara was very pleased.

They had some time before the bus required them to board, and Barbara asked what April wanted to do. April stood still, and thought for a while. Barbara laughed to herself to see this little girl so serious at making a decision. "Well, Barbara asked?"

"I am thinking," April replied. And Barbara almost laughed out loud. This little girl was not like any of her grandchildren. Her grandchildren were loud and noisy, boisterous, and bossy. Truthfully she loved them all, but they wore her out. They liked theme parks. Barbara said to herself the last time they had gone, leaving her exhausted, "I will never take them again."

They did not stay with her, they went darting all over that park. Barbara spent the entire day looking for them. She would find one or two. Then see others, and tell the two to say there. She would get the others, go back to where the two were supposed to be, and they would be gone. She was so frustrated and tired, she said she would never take them again.

But this little girl was like an old soul. She was patient, and thought things through before doing them. She would give her blunt opinion. Barbara was busting with anticipation to see what April would want to do in the two hours they had before boarding the bus.

"Have you any ideas?" Barbara asked her.

"I do, and I was hoping there are horses to ride nearby." That about floored Barbara.

"Horses," she said aloud. "You want to go on a horse ride? Dear me, I have not ridden on a horse since I was a little girl. Okay, I know where to go. Come on Taxi," Barbara hollered, and soon a yellow car pulled up beside them by the curb. Barbara opened the back door, both of them entered and sat down.

"Where to?" asked the driver.

"Take us to the riding academy. It's about a quarter mile from here. Are you familiar with it?" asked Barbara.

"Yes, I am," answered the driver. And in seconds they were driving off in another direction. April had no clue where they were headed, but she trusted Barbara. The driver drove very fast. Barbara was holding onto the arm of the door. They would slide to the left and right across the back seat as the driver went around turns.

April began to laugh, and the driver looked in his rearview mirror, but said nothing. In no time at all, they were there.

The riding academy was a very rundown place. It sure had changed over the years, thought Barbara. This used to be a very nice place - with flowers and fresh paint on the barn and rails. April noticed the shabby shape the barn was in. She knew it really needed a coat of painting, there were broken boards, doors listing on hinges that were broken, and high weeds around the buildings. But her heart almost took wing when she saw the horses. They were not shabby. They were in good shape, fat and happy.

One of the employees, a boy about sixteen came over to them asking, "What do you want?"

"She wants to ride." answered Barbara.

The boy began "We have some ponies to the side of the . . ."

April interrupted, "I don't want to ride a pony. I want to ride a horse." The boy looked surprised. And he came back with a sorrel mare that was about fourteen hands who was tacked up in western attire. April ducked under the rail to mount, and the boy said, "You have to pay first, and stay in the ring."

Barbara whistled to the boy, "I am paying, here," she said waving dollar bills.

The boy asked April if she needed help to get on, "Nope," she said. In one, two, three, she was up in the saddle. She instinctively picked up the reins, and asked, "Does she neck rein or is she single rein?"

"I don't know," said the boy. "She just came in a few days ago, no one has had her out yet, and I don't ride.

April thought to herself, "Well, we will find out. Won't we."

They began walking around the ring, the second time around was a trot, and then April reversed the direction. The mare was definitely neck reined. Then it was a canter, and it felt like so much fun. April could not hold back laughing. Then April gave the mare a good gut kick, and the mare went into a dead run. Watching her, Barbara felt afraid. She did not know if April could handle herself on that horse. The boy was afraid too. He just started this job the beginning of May. And he did not want to be fired because a kid was showing off, and got hurt.

April rounded that ring in a dead run, and slowed the mare after she completed the loop. That felt great! And soon they were back in "show mode," trotting and cantering. The mare began to snort as she made strides. April knew she was beginning to tire and to give. So she took her to the center of the ring for ground work. Stop, back, back, back and stop. That was good. Turn, turn, turn, turn, around and around, and after seven spins they stopped. April leaned forward, and patted the mare for her good behavior and obedience.

Barbara was astounded at the level of experience this little girl had riding. She seemed far too young to be so experienced on a horse she had never ridden before. April dismounted in the center of the ring, and Barbara was fascinated. Nothing could turn her head, she wanted to see what April knew and what she was doing. April walked and stopped. The mare followed her and stopped. April ran to the right and stopped. The mare then ran to the right, right beside April and stopped. April turned and caressed the mares head, and patted her side.

Barbara looked in the direction of the boy, and he was standing there with his mouth gaping open in disbelief at the mare and the little girl's ability.

There was someone else watching April. Marilee was in the big house, which had big windows that allowed a clear view of the ring. She was not a visitor at the academy. She was the daughter of Colonel Artie Becker, well known Olympian in the Equestrian competition for the U.S. team. She regretting telling her father she would come home and take care of old Roger, his last jumping horse. Roger had "saved the day" literally two years ago, and was spoiled by her father. He did not let just anyone take care of his horse. Marilee had an eye for talent - be it in real estate, horses, or riding, and this little girl had it. She had showmanship ability. With a few more years and training, there was no telling what this little girl would become. Marilee came out of the double doors to the balcony and hollered,

"Hello," which caught Barbara's attention, but she did not answer. Feeling a little irritated, the woman came down from the balcony, down the marble steps, onto the dirt driveway, to the ring side near Barbara. "Is that your little girl?" she asked.

"No, I am her Grandmother, sort of," said Barbara.

"She's quite good at riding, you know?" asked the woman.

"No, I did not know," answered Barbara, never taking her eyes off of April.

"I'd love to give you my card. I specialize in training children to ride professionally," said the woman.

"Well, okay," said Barbara, and the woman handed Barbara a business card with fancy lettering on it. Barbara put the card in her pocket. As the two women stood there watching April. who by now was back on riding, testing the mare. April had the mare cantering again. April hung on the side "trick riding," and, as they passed the women, you could not see April at all. Soon April was pooped and stopped the mare. She slid off of the mare's rump onto the ground. She then walked to the mare. And lightly touching the mare's nose, she pulled on the reins, and the mare went into a kneeling position.

April spoke to the mare. Neither of the women could hear what April was saying, and soon the mare laid over on her side, as if sleeping or dead. April laid the reins on the mare, and walked completely around the horse. The mare never moved. As April finished walking around the horse, she stood back and said very loudly, "Up," and the mare stood, and shook herself. The boy clapped his hands and laughed. He was quite amazed. Barbara was speechless

The woman said, "Do contact me when you get home. I am very interested in her."

That is when Barbara said, "Well, I hate to disappoint you, but this little girl is on her way to California to be with her Aunt. Her Mother is sickly, and I am not sure if she will return to her home, or stay in California. So for that reason, I cannot tell you one way or another. I am not really her Grandmother. I am only her temporary Grandmother on our bus trip, and we must leave soon." Looking at her watch Barbara said, "Oh, dear, April. April come quick," she hollered. "We really must go."

April led the mare to the boy, and thanked him. He tipped his cap towards her. April ducked under the board of the coral. Then she ran to join Barbara taking her hand in hers.

The taxi had just pulled in the lane, filling it with dust. "Okay folks, get in and I'll have you back in no time." Barbara shuddered at the thought of riding with this driver again. As they sat back, hanging on, Barbara stroked April's hair, "You are sure full of surprises, aren't you?"

"Who, me?" questioned April.

"Yes, you dear. You are quite a good rider. Did you know that?"

"Yes," said April. "I love to ride. I rode a lot on our farm. I had lots of horses teach me, and Momma did too. Did I tell you my Momma was Native American?" Barbara just hugged her. And she felt tears welling up in her eyes. She could only imagine the heartfelt pain this little girl's Mother had sending her away.

As the taxi pulled out of the driveway, the riding academy woman impressed the image of the small girl in her mind. She was very good at recalling faces, and this one was easy. She hoped that one day they would meet again. And with a talent like that, at such a young age, she could train that girl into a world class rider. Well, maybe she thought. It was worth a try. She went back up the steps into the house, and made a telephone call.

Soon Barbara and April were back at the place where they started. Barbara paid the taxi man, and they walked very fast to the bus where there was a line of people boarding. "We are good. We are not late," Barbara said out of breath. As they stood in line, Barbara slipped the business card into April's hand, "Keep this," she said. "Tuck it away in a safe place so it is never lost."

Barbara hugged April from behind. And she whispered in her ear, "I am so proud of you, dear little one. You ride like the wind. You sure surprised me, and it was a good wish of what to do. And she hugged her again, and April beamed.

As they boarded the bus, April sat in her usual seat. Ed stood to check who was or who was not on the bus. Soon he sat in his seat, and got the microphone for the bus. "Is everyone on. Is no one missing? Look around please."

The people on the bus began to put their thumbs up in the air, as if to say, "It's okay, everyone is on, and we are all okay.

Ed sat down and started the engine. Soon they began to pull out of the parking area. This was a great stop. April learned a lot here. She liked Maryland, and maybe someday she would come back. Little did she know that she indeed would come back. Someday was just a few short years away, but not yet, not yet!

She had far to go to reach California, to this illusive Aunt with no name, only a town name. April did not care. She had no worries, she had such a fun day. Her belly was still full, and she was happy, truly happy.

As she began to feel sleepy, she realized how smart her two brothers were to send her on this trip. She did not know how they knew, but she knew they loved her to send her away. The bus was fully dark now, most everyone was asleep. She looked at Ed the bus driver, and wondered how did he do it. How did he stay awake both day and night, follow the driving schedule, and make sure they were safe? And soon she was asleep. Ed looked in his rearview mirror to look at his passengers. Lastly he saw April, asleep. The hue of blue on her eyelids closed tight, and he smiled.

April woke up before most of the passengers. Ed noticed, and said, "Well, you're up awfully early."

April acknowledged his comment by saying, "Yes, I usually wake up early," while rubbing the sleep from her eyes. With that, she slipped off her seat to the back of the bus, and to the bathroom. In and out, she did not want to spend much time in there.

April sat on her seat, rummaging in the back pack, and pulled out her brush. She began to brush her hair. "Gosh, I need to wash my hair," she thought to herself, "and a bath would feel good too." She had on the same clothes as when she first boarded the bus, days ago. But she did not know when, or how that was going to happen, as her life was on that bus.

As they drove along, one by one passengers awoke, and slowly the bus became lively again. Ed reached for his mic and began to speak. "People, we crossed through Virginia last night while you were sleeping. We will be making a stop in Kentucky. I know some of you will be getting off there, and not rejoining us." And a cheer came from the back of the bus. Ed continued, "We may have to change buses in Kentucky. I am not sure just yet, since I have not heard from my dispatcher. But either way, we are traveling at a good speed, and I expect to be stopping around ten o'clock this morning." Ed put the receiver back into the mount and sighed.

April wondered about changing buses. Was Ed no longer going to be on the bus, or would they be transferring their things to another bus with Ed. She did not ask. She sat there, and peeled open a hardboiled egg she had squirreled away. She made sure none of the egg shell fell anywhere but on her napkin. As she munched, Ed handed back to her a small cardboard container that had red marking on it, "Here," he said. "Have one on me." And as April took it, she was sure it was milk. How handy is that? she thought. And as she struggled to open the top of the container, it opened. April took a drink, and it sure was milk, very cold and delicious. She was a happy camper. She sat there eating her boiled egg and drinking the milk Ed gave to her. She was soon finished, and carefully folded her napkin, making sure she didn't drop any crumbs. Then she put all the garbage inside the now empty milk carton while she sat watching the cars go by quietly.

As they continued along, a passenger came front to speak to Ed. It was an older man from the back of the bus. April could not hear all of the conversation, but the man was wondering how long the "down" time would be. Ed told him that he would know more once they pulled into the bus station in Kentucky. Satisfied, the man left to go back to his seat.

On and on they went. April saw many white fences and green pastures. April would get excited each time she saw

a horse, and making sounds of "Ohhhhh" or "Ouuuuuu".
Ed just chuckled at her. "So you are a horse lover?" Ed
asked April.

"Yes I am," April replied.

There were many horse farms in Kentucky. They all
seemed so nice, with painted fences, and the horses all
looked fat and healthy. Some had foals at their side. The
foals were funny. Some stayed with their Moms, and some
were playing with other foals. They looked so silly - running
and chasing one another, tearing around in the pastures.
April wondered if her Aunt had horses, or if she lived in
the city. She hoped that her Aunt was like her Mother,
loving horses. April would do all she could do to help her.
She wondered if she had cousins. And if they were nice,
or played tricks on each other. She was full of questions as
they crossed each state. There was so much she did not
know, but she felt she would take each day one at a time.
There was no sense in trying to figure out the future. It
would come anyway, and whether they were good times or
problems, she would see it all then.

April pulled out her small blue suitcase and a piece of
paper and a pencil. She closed the suitcase so it would not
spill its contents, and, using it as a desk, she began to make
a list. April loved to draw and make lists that only she could
understand. As she wrote, there were very few letters as
she could not read very well. She wanted to arrive at her
Aunt's home with flowers, so April wrote what she heard in
sounding out the word flower. She wrote "FLOR", and drew
a picture of a flower. This was a reminder paper of things
she should do. As she continued her "list", she became lost
in time. Before too long the bus began to slow and turned
off onto a ramp. April opened her small blue suitcase and
put her list and pencil inside. She closed it up tight, placing
it on the floor. This must be their next stop.

The bus continued on, not far from the ramp and there
was the bus station. There had to be one hundred buses

there, under cover of a hanger shed. It Allowed the buses to drive out or back up without a wall in front or back. "What an amazing thing," April thought.

As Ed pulled the bus onto the blacktop of the bus station; he pulled his mic off again to make an announcement. "People, we have a slight change of plans. Our bus is in need of repairs. Some of you may continue on with another bus if you choose. Snd those of you who choose to stay one full day, may do so at the expense of our travel line. There is a hotel near the bus line, and you are welcome to stay there.

Barbara was trying frantically to get April's attention, when a passenger behind April tapped on April's shoulder. "Excuse me," he said. "Someone is trying to get your attention." April turned her head to see Barbara motioning for her to come to her. April got up and walked the aisle to Barbara.

"Come and sit with me," Barbara said, moving some of her things out of the way to make room.

"Are you going to change buses to continue on to your Aunt's home in California, or do you want to stay in a motel, get a shower, and wash your clothing?

April did not have to think long. "Oh, I need to wash my hair," she said.

And Barbara said, "Okay, you stay with me. I will be your Grandma again. Okay, you scoot and get your things ready. Then listen to what the bus driver says." April scooted back to her seat.

As the bus stopped making big air screeching sounds, it came to a full stop. Ed stood up and announced. "Listen up. Those of you who want to continue on your trip to your destination, go to the carts on the left side of our bus. The handlers will remove your luggage under the bus as you tell them, and you will be boarded on another bus onto your destination. Please do not forget to take what you have here on this bus with you. Take your time, look around, and take all of your things. We cannot be responsible for things you leave behind."

"For those of you who want to stay over for one night, and leave at ten o'clock in the morning, you go to the carts on the right. They will take your luggage to your hotel room and escort you with a ride. Those who are staying overnight, please take all of your things you have with you on this bus to the carts. Pack it all up. Put it in a bag or whatever. If you leave it behind, it will be put in the trash."

April slipped her backpack on her back holding her tiger under one arm. She carried her little blue suitcase handle in her left hand. She was ready. April motioned for Ed to come to her and bend down. "Thank you for taking care of me, Ed," she said and kissed his cheek. Ed stood up as the travelers teased him.

"Okay, okay," Ed announced. "Travelers wanting to continue on, you may exit the bus now." Many of the bus passengers got off of the bus. Some were loaded with bags with handles, and small suitcases. Some grumbled, and some were happy as they got off of the bus. They went to the left where a long train of sorts was waiting. Passengers went to a seat, and placed what they had with them. Then they went back to "our" bus. Meanwhile a crew member unlocked the bottom half of the bus, opening it up. There inside the belly of the bus was a lot of luggage. Each passenger took turns showing the crew member a ticket that identified their luggage. It took a while, but soon all of them had the right luggage. Next they were getting on the long train to another bus under that covered shed.

"Okay," Ed announced. "The rest of you are staying, you may exit the bus now." Then Ed clicked off his receiver.

"So you are staying behind?" Ed asked.

"Oh, yes I am. I want to take a bath and wash my hair," April said.

And Ed chuckled. "Are you staying with Barbara?"

"Yes, I am," answered April.

"You made a good choice," Ed said.

As Barbara came down the bus aisle, she stopped to take April with her, "Ready?" she asked. April nodded yes and down the steps they went, to the long carts. They both got to a seat and Barbara told April to stay there, she had to claim her luggage. It did not take long. There were only a small number of people - seven all together. April counted them, and they rode the little train of carts to the bus station office. A woman came out, writing down names, and soon the little train drove them to a hotel. It was a very big house, and the parking lot was full of cars, too many to count.

At the hotel, Barbara and April got off of the train cart, as did the other people. They watched as porters came out of the hotel, and one by one a porter came to each rider asking which luggage was theirs. Then they took their suitcase, sometimes two or three, carrying them into the hotel with the passenger following them.

The porters were well-dressed young men and women, in red suits with black striping. They each wore a big hat, white gloves, and white long stockings with black shoes. It was easy to spot a porter, They all dressed alike.

Barbara had two large suitcases which the porter carried, and a small overnight suitcase which she carried. April had carried her own things, and easily followed them.

As they entered the hotel, it almost took April's breath away. There was deep, plush carpeting on the floor. Everything was either white or painted with gold. There was a huge chandelier over their heads at the center of the room - the glass of the hanging tiers shined like crystals. April could not help her awe and staring at the beautiful hotel. Barbara had to take her hand, and pull her along. As they came to the guest registry, it was a big desk that was much taller than April. Barbara could barely put her arms up on top to sign in. The man behind the desk was very polite. He handed Barbara a card, and motioned for the porter to escort Barbara with her luggage to the room. "219," Barbara said, and April mimicked her.

They came to the edge of that big room to a gold-lined box of sorts. There the porter pressed a button and big doors opened. The porter and Barbara stepped inside, April just stood there. "Come on in," said Barbara. "Don't be afraid. You know what an elevator is, don't you?"

April shook her head no. it was obvious to Barbara April was afraid. "Wait a minute," she said to the porter. Barbara went out of the elevator, and took April by the hand. "April, you do trust me. Don't you?" she asked.

April answered her, "Yes, I do, but what will happen when we go in there?"

Barbara explained that the box took them up faster than stairs. It was an elevator that could take a load in less than a minute. April again looked at that box. The porter motioned for her to come in. She took Barbara hand balancing her Tiger under her arm, and on they went.

The elevator went up. She could feel it moving up, sort of like a ride. But you could only see the walls, nothing else. Then very quickly, the elevator stopped and the door opened automatically. They all stepped off and the porter turned to the left. They passed two doors, and the third door was 219.

Barbara leaned over, and inserted a card. The door made a buzzing noise, an unlock noise. Then Barbara turned the door handle, and they were in their room. The porter put the luggage inside the room, and stood there like a soldier. Barbara reached into her purse, and handed the porter two dollar bills. Then the porter left closing the door behind him.

The room was much bigger than April ever could have imagined. Why it was bigger than the whole downstairs of their house on the farm combined. The room had two really big beds, a small refrigerator, a TV on the wall, and a huge window. You could look out and see the highway and beyond. To the far end of the room was a big bathroom. It had a bath tub, a shower, and a whole ten more steps to the toilet. It was amazing, clean, fancy and so big.

Barbara put her luggage on a long stool that easily held both pieces of her luggage. She opened them up and pulled out some articles of clothing. She looked at April, and said, "Put your suitcase and backpack over there on the other stool."

April did so, and then Barbara told her to get out her dirty clothing. April just stood there, and said, "I don't have any. Except the ones I have on."

Barbara realized that April had been on the bus for three days, and did not have a place to wash up or change her clothing. "Okay, Toots," Barbara said. "You go in the tub and wash. I will send our things to the laundry."

April was excited to get washed. She longed to wash her hair which felt stiff. April went into the bathroom, and began to run the water into the big tub. As she did, she undressed and got into that tub of warm water. Ah, it was so nice. Barbara came in and took her soiled clothing. She handed her some shampoo and soap.

April scrubbed her hair and body until she felt clean all over. She stepped out onto a thick, luxurious towel the hotel provided, and buried her face into the softness. She found a smaller towel and wrapped it around her head and hair to make a turban to dry her hair. She wrapped the larger towel around her, and opened the door.

Barbara was sitting on a bed, and told her to come over. She took the turban towel off of April's head and sprayed something on her hair. It was to take out tangles. And it did a good job. Barbara combed through April's hair. It was long, almost to the bottom of her shoulders. "You have such beautiful hair, and I declare I believe it is curling," said Barbara.

"Now, I have something for you to wear." And Barbara held up a pretty dress with all colors of flowers print on it, and the sleeves were puffy and short. She also had a small white slip. April was so excited.

Barbara held the slip up and April stepped forward putting her head into the hole, and down it came. The slip was cotton, so soft. Then came the dress. Once on, Barbara said, "turn around." She then zipped up the zipper to the back of April's neck. "Now turn around. I want to see what you look like dressed like a girl." April did and Barbara was very pleased. April felt pretty. She liked dressing up, but on the farm the only time she wore a dress was for church.

"Now you can watch television or entertain yourself until I am clean, alright?" Barbara told her. April nodded her head in agreement, and Barbara disappeared into the bathroom shutting the door.

She did not turn on the TV. She preferred to sit there and soak in the room, and listen to Barbara. April could hear singing coming from the bathroom. It was Barbara, and she had a pretty singing voice.

April recognized the tune and sang along quietly. *"Doe a deer a female deer, Sew a needle and some thread."* It was a song from a record she played on her record player at home. April really liked Barbara, and hoped that she would not be leaving the bus anytime soon. No one had ever been this nice to her.

April pushed those thoughts far from her mind. She was determined to enjoy the time they had together. April never had a living Grandmother. Well she did, but that woman was plain mean to her. Barbara was kind, and such fun to be with.

Soon Barbara was out dressed in a pretty turquoise colored top and pants. She had on a white pearl necklace with matching earrings and white sandals. April looked down at her scruffy sneakers, and hid them under her chair by crossing her legs. Barbara saw it, and said, "We are going to fix that when we get out of here."

And true to her word, she called a cab. They went to a shoe store. There she bought April the prettiest white shoes with a strap that went over the top of her foot to close, and a white pair of socks with lace at the top. April had never imagined or hoped to have nice things like this, and she hugged Barbara.

"Okay," said Barbara. "How about we get out of here, and look around?" They went out of the store, carefully closing the door so it would lock. Outside they chose to walk around. They went down the stairs back to the hotel. They noticed toward the front of the hotel there was an interesting elevator, one that was like a bubble. That elevator was glass with a floor that allowed you to see all over - left, right and center from high above. "We are definitely taking that ride when we come back in, eh?" said Barbara.

"Yes," said April with delight.

They headed toward the shopping center of the hotel. Right away April saw a dress just like hers, and realized this is where Barbara must have gone when April was taking her bath. And she felt such gratitude in her heart. She wanted to be extra obedient and loving to Barbara for being so kind to her. And she did, and it was not difficult for her. She had a kindness, a gentle kindness, that she learned from someone she loved, and thought about that every day.

They went to hail a cab and decided to go into town. There were many shops, restaurants, clothing stores, and Barbara spotted a movie theatre. "April, would you enjoy going to the movies?" Barbara asked.

April had not seen many movies. The ones she did "see", she watched from the floor of the movie theatre. She would come home with gum and jujubes on her clothing and in her hair. "How did you get this?" her Mother asked one evening.

"I was afraid. The monster movies scare me." So the most she ever saw were Saturday Matinees with vampires, werewolves or the hideous creatures. There were always screaming teenagers in these movies, and they always had people running afraid.

She did not enjoy them, but Mother always reminded the boys, "Take your sister along." So there she would sit in the front row. And it seemed that when the vampires were going to take a bite, it was her neck. So she would slither down in her seat, and lay on the floor.

"April, what kind of movies do you like?" Barbara asked.

April really did not know what to say, so she said what she did know. "I don't want to see any monster movies, vampires, or werewolves. Barbara's eyes widened with disbelief that a six-year-old girl would know about them.

"Oh, I don't like those kinds of movies either," Barbara replied. So, at the movie theatre, they each had tickets to see a nature movie. It was a re-run of a favorite of Barbara's. April genuinely enjoyed that movie. She particularly liked the rabbit and the skunk. That made April laugh. She did not like the sad parts, and she held onto Barbara's arm, once burying her head into Barbara's sweater.

Barbara knew April had a tender heart towards animals, and she was pleased. She too was like that with her cats and her dog. The popcorn and soda April barely touched. April was not a big eater for being such a strong little girl. She was more of a grazer. Barbara tossed the popcorn and sodas in the trash as they exited the movie theatre.

Throughout the day, April would repeat things from the movie, not in imitation, but teaching moments. Such as, "What did I tell you while the skunk would drag his foot from side to side as if embarrassed, answering his Mother. Kindness matters. You like being kind. Don't you? So I want you to be kind to others," and April would smile. Barbara was genuinely pleased that April enjoyed that movie, as all children should. She was beginning to love this little girl, and it surprised her a little. She had a small talk with herself, privately without words. Barbara you are fifty-nine years old with eleven grandchildren that drive you batty. A husband that you love, but works too much. Most times your own children come to visit, but it is for a meal or to borrow something, and that something is usually money. So enjoy this little girl that asks for so little, and gives back so much. Your time with her will be short. Tennessee is your next stop, and that is your home.

Barbara looked at April as they walked through the mall, hoping April could not read her face of concern. Being a child April was walking along looking at everything, the clothing, the pictures, the stairs and elevators, and the big displays that ran the length of the mall. She was a bright little girl that did not miss much.

At the music store April stopped, lingering. "Do you want to go inside?" Barbara asked. April looked at her shaking her head in the affirmative. Inside they went, and April sat down on the piano bench. She placed her fingers on the keys, and began playing a little tune. Barbara was blown away. "When did this little girl learn this, and who taught her?" she wondered silently to herself.

There was no one in the music store when they went in. Barbara did not even see a clerk. So as April played, Barbara kept her eyes looking around, hoping this was okay for April to play this beautiful instrument. She did not want to get April or herself into trouble.

As April played the little tune, a sales woman came nearby and asked, "How old is your Granddaughter?"

"Here we go again," thought Barbara, but answered, "Six, she is six years old." The clerk watched April play. Although her fingers were small, she was able to stretch them to the keys. She searched for, but could not reach the pedals at the bottom of the piano. It was obvious that April had to have lessons, and it was obvious that April must have practiced a lot to have remembered the notes and keys so well. But she was so young.

As April concentrated, looking left and right searching for the right keys, she was playing from memory. It was sort of comical to the clerk, but people began to notice. And one by one, they entered the music store. Many watched April play, smiling. Some made kind remarks, but they also looked around, and some made purchases. When April was finished playing that tune, she broke into another that many of the customers were familiar with. And as April sang, they all began to sing along. April looked up in surprise, but did not stop playing or singing. She smiled a huge smile. Here right in front of her was a party of sorts. At the end of that song, April stood up, placed her hands by the sides of her dress, and curtsied. Barbara was impressed. The people clapped and April smiled. She went to Barbara and said, "We can go now, okay?" and Barbara hugged her. They left the music store saying, "Excuse me, pardon me," over and over, because the sight of seeing a little girl playing the piano and singing brought in many, many people into the music store.

"Well, that was something," Barbara said with a smile on her face. "Do you have any more surprises for me?" and April reached over and hugged her. They enjoyed their day together walking all around.

By six o'clock, they were both hungry, and Barbara had noticed a nice restaurant along the way back. They hailed a cab because Barbara's feet began to hurt. The new shoes she had purchased were not broken in, and she wanted to rest from walking. April on the other hand never seemed to get tired.

The restaurant was of Italian cuisine. Barbara thought April might enjoy some pizza, chicken fingers, or something like that. Barbara was hungry. She knew she wanted spaghetti and meatballs with garlic bread, or garlic knots, and a big tall glass of sweetened ice tea.

As the waiter took them to their table, he said his name was Michael, and he handed them their menus to look at.

April sat there and asked Barbara "What are you going to have?" Barbara told her, and April said, "I'll have that too."

Barbara was surprised, and asked April, "Would you like pizza?" April shook her head No. "Chicken tenders?"

April said, "I don't know what they are, but I sure like bisketti," and Barbara smiled.

"Well then, bisketti you shall have," said Barbara.

The food came promptly, and the dishes were huge! The spaghetti was cooked to perfection, not soggy, the meatballs were tender and big, and the sauce was perfect. April's eyes got so big when she saw the big order. She said, "I will try to eat all of it, but I'm not so sure."

Barbara said, "You eat what you can. Don't feel like you have to eat all of that. We can always take what you are unable to eat along back with us." So they both dug in, and Barbara was amused at April trying to twirl the spaghetti on her fork. Then she bent down with her head, gathered up the noodles with her mouth and sucked them into her small mouth. Some of them would ooze along, and leave a trail of sauce on her cheeks.

It was obvious April was enjoying her *bisketti* and meatballs, but she had not touched the garlic knots. "April would you like to try the bread?"

"No thanks," April said. "I don't like the smell of them. They are like flower," and she smiled.

"What a little stinker she is," thought Barbara. Oh, how she wished she could take April to her home to meet her grandchildren, husband, sons and daughters. She was such a little delight. But how could she let April's Aunt know that she would be delayed?"

"April, would you like to come home with me for a little while to meet my family?"

April looked up at Barbara, and said, "Sure I would, but what about my ticket. Maybe they won't let me take the rest of my trip to my Auntie's home."

"Oh, sure they will," said Barbara. "I have changed plans before. It's a little bit more money, but don't you worry about that. I would gladly pay the difference for you to come to our home. I know my husband would love to meet you. He would be disappointed if I would told him all about you, and he would not have a chance to meet you."

April smiled, "Okay. I think I would like that," she said. And just like that, that is how April's plans changed.

They did not have much to take home in their boxes. As the taxi took them home, it was obvious April was now tired. They arrived at their hotel about 7 o'clock, and drug themselves to their hotel. They took the bubble glass elevator to the top. April's tired eyes gleamed with interest as the elevator slowly went up. She gasped and pointed, "look you can see the sun setting. And the moon is like a fingernail."

"Oh, you are right," said Barbara as they went back down to their floor.

Barbara knew all too well that their time together was going to come to an end. She delighted at having her "New Granddaughter" come to her home, and be spoiled a bit by her and her husband. But when she would leave, there would definitely be a void in their lives. She was that special and lovable.

Soon they were at their hotel room, Barbara searched for their hotel card, swiping it, the door lock clicked, Barbara turned the knob and they were inside.

They were both tired. April began to undress, hanging her dress and slip carefully on the back of the chair by her bedside. April removed her shoes, then her socks. She shook her socks out, and hung them with her clothes. She put her shoes carefully halfway under her bed. Then searched her backpack for her pajamas, and put them on.

Someone taught this little girl much. May God bless her Mother, and watch over her. And make her well. This little thing must have been loved. Barbara was overcome with emotion and began to sniff. "Are you getting a cold?" April asked.

"No, silly girl. I was just watching you undress, and put your things away so carefully. Who taught you that?"

"My brothers," April said. Barbara was shocked, she was sure it was her Mother, but this answer confirmed that April's Mother was sick. So sick that siblings taught her much of what she knew.

She thought to herself, that she was going to suggest they should pray together, that maybe, maybe April would offer answers in that manner.

Barbara changed in the bathroom, and freshened up. Her feet were sore, and the top of her foot had red marks where the straps of her shoes went. It was a relief to get them off. Barbara was not as careful with her shoes as her little companion. She tossed them into a corner as she came out of the bathroom wearing her nightgown.

"April, do you say prayers at night?"

"Sure I do," said April.

"Well then, come on over here. I would love to say prayers with you." April came to Barbara's side of the bed, and kneeled down with her arms on the top of the bed. Barbara did the same, although her knees were going to suffer for this. "Do you want me to pray for us?" asked Barbara.

"No, that's fine. I know how," said April. And as she prayed, her words were filled with thanks to God. But she did not reveal much about her family other than asking God to keep them safe. She was very emotional. Tears began to roll down her cheeks when she said, "I love you Heavenly Father. I really do." Barbara rubbed April's side to assure her it was okay, and soon April said, "Amen."

It was now Barbara turn. She was not long in prayers. She was quite brief, thanking God for her little companion. And asking him to assure April that all would be well for her, as she said, "Amen." April had fallen asleep beside her with her head turned towards Barbara. She noticed that April's little button red lips looked so sweet, her eyes almost had a shadow of light blue on her eyelids, with blonde and brown in her eyelashes.

April was such a picture of peace. Barbara did not want to move her just yet. She wanted to enjoy this small moment a little longer. It had been such a long, long time since her own daughter was this little. She was a grown woman with four children of her own now. Where did the time go? Time seems to fly when you least want it to. Barbara enjoyed being an active Mother of five rambunctious young children. There were trips, vacations, school adventures, sports, cheerleading, and athletics. Well it seemed like an endless merry-go-round, often leaving Barbara stressed for decent dinners and time with her husband. Barbara loved her husband so much. This trip he gave to her was a gift. She had talked about going to Maine for a long time. She was born and raised there, and she wanted to return for a reunion. What a wonderful time she had. Her responsibilities were at home. Tennessee was her home with her family, not Maine.

Barbara cooked ten days of meals for her husband, but she knew he would most likely order out, and she smiled to herself. Yeah, she was the lucky one. She had a one-in-a-million man. Her two daughters were married, well, the one on her second marriage. She would often be concerned for them. But rarely said anything other than, "So, how are you? How are things going?"The answers were always vague, and she left it at that. They obviously did not want her to know, and it was none of her business - unless they wanted it to be.

Barbara stood, her knees cracking, and she groaned as she bent over picking April up to put her into her own bed. With one hand she pulled the covers down, and the other held on to April. Once in bed, Barbara said to herself, "Well Barbara, you still have it," and she laughed to herself.

Sleep came easy to Barbara. She was at peace. April slept soundly, she never heard Barbara get up to go to the bathroom. April did not hear anything. She was dreaming of being with her brothers. They were making mud pies and laughing. They were pretending they were at a fancy restaurant, making cherry pies with mud. She slept with a smile on her face. The two companions were swept into dreamland with happy thoughts. They were both tired and completely at rest. The alarm woke them both too early. It startled Barbara, she did not want to wake April so abruptly. She looked at April's bed, and it was empty. Barbara shot straight up, looking around. There was April, all dressed in her "traveling clothes" with her hair up in a pony tail, just sitting there quietly.

"Are you alright? Barbara asked.

"Yes, I am" April replied. "I did not want to wake you. so I was very quiet."

"Do you always get up early?" asked Barbara.

"Yes, I do. I was born and raised on a dairy farm. I would wake up very early to walk to the barn to go to my Momma," April told her.

"Ahh, a small insight into this little one's life," thought Barbara, "it will come, little by little." Normally she would not care, but this girl was . . . so little, so innocent. She was special. Yes, now she admitted that fact to herself. She cared about her maybe too much, but she could not help herself. She was excited to take April to Tennessee to her home, to be with her and her family for a little while.

The two of them left their rooms and headed to the hotel's basement floor where there was a full restaurant.

Barbara kept her eye on her wrist watch. They had to be at the bus terminal by 9 o'clock. It was now 8 o'clock.

They had scrambled eggs, bacon and a muffin. Barbara had tea and, April had chocolate milk. They both chatted awhile, but were mindful that they could not chat the time away. So they both ate heartily and left. "It was so nice of the bus company to pick up our tab for everything while we were here," Barbara said.

April did not understand, and when Barbara explained what she said to her, April thought they should have done more. Barbara laughed at her, and swiped at her back side to tease her. April ran laughing.

The bus terminal was a busy place. There were more people on this bus than when they came in on the last one. April searched for Ed. "their" bus driver. Soon Ed came around the corner of the bus with a clipboard under his arm wearing his company hat. "Okay people, let's board," he said. He pulled at April's pigtail, and winked at her. And soon the bus was pulling out, heading to Tennessee. April sat in her usual seat, and Barbara sat right behind her. Barbara wanted April to agree to come to their home and she must say something soon.

As Barbara sat behind April, she told April she would love for her to come and stay with her and her husband for two weeks or so. April thought it would be fun, and April said she would.

Barbara was concerned that the Aunt in California might mind. After all, the Aunt did not know Barbara. And maybe she had to work around the bus schedule to pickup April. If only there was a way to call or contact this Aunt of April's. But April said she did not know the address. and the bus ticket only revealed the bus station name - no identifying person.

After questioning April, Barbara spoke to Ed about this. Ed contacted his supervisor at the Tennessee station. Ed was told that an extension would be allowed for an additional cost. Which Barbara said was fine, and so Ed took care of all of the necessary details. But Ed, too, was concerned as to how to let April's Aunt in California know that April would be staying at a home for two weeks, and would not be arriving the fourth of May as her ticket showed.

All Ed could and did do is notify the dispatcher, and then the supervisor would forward a message to the bus station in Fresno, California. If word was left there, surely when the Aunt would come to retrieve April, she would be told about the schedule change. Or perhaps the station manager would know April's Aunt, and call her or make a stop to her home. Let her know that her niece was staying two weeks for a little vacation, and then resuming the bus trip to her in California.

When the information was gathered, a telegraph was dispatched to the bus station in Fresno, California.

Both Barbara and April talked in anticipation of their time together in Tennessee with Barbara's family. There was Barbara's husband Tom, her sons - Luke, Adam, Jay, Robert or Bob (they had been twins, jay-bob), and her daughters - Linda and Ann. These names had no meaning to April, other than they were special to Barbara. April paid close attention to details of each one as Barbara spoke about them all. April would just have to wait to meet the grandsons to know who they all were, there were too many.

It seemed like a long, long time to reach Tennessee. For some unknown reason, there was a lot of traffic. Not just cars, but tractor trailer trucks as well. The road was full, and Ed had to take extra care while driving. April was determined NOT to be a distraction to Ed.

April pulled out her suitcase, and got a pencil and paper. She began to think about what she wanted to do when she arrived in California. Barbara watched her, then she too had a notepad and pen, and began writing. The two went on and on for almost an hour, deep in thought and writing. Barbara flipped her pad closed, clicked her pen shut, and put them both away. April looked up at her, and Barbara asked if she could help April. April handed Barbara her paper with the list.

"Let me see. You want to find your home, and then maybe ride horses, go swimming, and help your Aunt clean? Is that right? You want to clean her house?" April nodded her head yes. "Help to plant flowers, and walk the dog. Do you know if she has a dog April? April shook her head no. Barbara took the list, folded it carefully, and said, "Do you know what I think?"

April said, "No. What do you think?" She smiled with her impish grin.

Barbara went on, "I think I would not have any expectations. You can't plan when you do not know where she lives, or who lives with her. So make it easy on yourself. Expect nothing, and you will be pleased." April smiled at Barbara. She was so smart. April wondered why her own family was not as kind and nice as Barbara was. And she was not even family.

Barbara leaned her head to the side against the window. She put her sweater between her head and the window, and nodded off. April leaned against Barbara, putting her head on Barbara's hip and stomach, and curling up her legs onto the seat. Soon Barbara's arm came down around April's back. It was such a nice feeling. And soon the two were fast asleep.

They slept until the bus slowed, and turned into the Tennessee bus terminal. When the bus lights came on, Barbara woke April, and they gathered their things. As they exited the bus, a man came forward with his arms outstretched, and Barbara walked into them. April just stood there until Barbara came to her. Barbara took her hand, and said, "April, this is my husband, Tom."

Tom was a medium-height man, amd very stout. Tom had glasses, greying hair, and very large strong hands. He outstretched his hand, and said, "Hello, April. So glad you are staying with us for a while. May I take your bags?"

April was touched, but said, "No thanks. I got them." And she carried her things to their silver Ford Caravan. Tom pulled the side door open, put Barbara's two bags in, and then her carry on. He looked at April, she handed him the back pack and suitcase, but held onto her tiger.

"You got a good traveling companion there, I see. He doesn't make any noise, never wants to eat, or complain," and he smiled at April. She climbed into the back seat, and buckled up. On route to their home, Barbara and Tom chatted about things - what she saw at the reunion, and people who asked about him. Then he told her about things that had happened at their home.

Tom looked into his rear view mirror and asked April, "Do you think want to do anything special while you are here with us, April?"

April said, "Being with Barbara and you is special to me." Tom looked at Barbara, and she winked at him.

Within an hour they were "home". They unloaded their things from the van. Then a dog came bounding outside to greet Barbara. "Oh, tootsie, Oh, tootsie. It's alright. Momma is home now. Come on, and come here." The little dog crouched down almost flat on the sidewalk, and Barbara picked her up. "This is our little Tootsie. She was a rescue dog at our local shelter. She was abused, so she is shy. She is also blind in one eye, but she gets along good, and she knows we love her." April came a step or two closer, and Tootsie began to smell her feet and socks. Tootsie's tail began to wag. She looked up at April, and began to bark.

April leaned over. and said, "Come here girl. I won't hurt you. I will pet, and love on you though." Tootsie came to April with her tongue hanging out and tail wagging.

"Boy, you sure won her over easily. She does not take to people that fast." said Tom. Inside went the four of them with Tootsie in the rear wagging her tail, and looking all around not wanting to miss a thing.

Barbara and Tom had a lovely home. It was very long, with stone on the outside. Inside it was big. The ceiling went way high, and had beams of wood. Tom said, "This is our ranch home, April. We had another home in town, but Barbara and I wanted a home without stairs. But it had to be big enough for all of our children and grandchildren. And this house sure is big!"

Barbara took April to a room that was to be for her and her alone. Barbara took some pillows off of the bed, and placed April's backpack on the chair close to the door. "There now. I think that will do. Come out, and let's you and I make some lunch, April. I know there are some leftovers in the refrigerator and odds and ends." April followed her to a big Kitchen with a counter as long as the kitchen itself. Barbara opened the refrigerator, and pulled out some meat, cheeses, grapes, tomatoes, and some boiled eggs. And finally she got some crackers from the cupboard.

"Tom," she called.

"I am right here. I am coming," he said. The three of them sat down and nibbled. Meanwhile they talked, not about anything specific, but more time to get to know one another.

Barbara's eyes gleamed as April held her own in the conversation with Tom. "So what do you do for work?" April asked Tom.

"I am a dentist," Tom answered. "I also assist other Doctors with oral surgeries." April had been to a dentist, and she did not like hers at all. At six, most all of her teeth had fillings. It was not because she had cavities, but because there was insurance money to be had in drilling and filling. She was half Native American and they have the most durable and hardest teeth. Still, she had all of her teeth filled. Once her dentist had dropped the drill in her mouth tearing her mouth badly. So she did not like dentists at all. Tom sensed something wrong, and he asked April. She bluntly told him.

"Oh, whoa," Tom said. "I would never do such a thing to you or anyone else. I am so sorry that happened to you, dear." April believed him.

"Do dentists make a lot of money?" she asked unabashedly. Tom looked at Barbara whose eyes were twinkling with mischief. "They do. They do, but we have to go to school for a long time. And we must also know a lot about people's teeth," Tom answered. Then he added, "I am going to let Tootsie out for a little bit," and he left the room.

April realized she had been personal, and it was not appropriate. She said, "Barbara, I did not mean to offend Mr. Tom. I am sorry."

Barbara began to clean up, and she said, "April, if Tom did not want to have a conversation with you, or answer you, he would not. I think if you want to apologize to him, then you need to do so."

April hopped off of her chair, and went to find Tom. He was outside watching Tootsie. April opened the big door, and walked right up to Tom. "Mr. Tom, I am very sorry for talking so fresh. I did not mean to be so nosey. I was just curious. You see, I am not sure what I want to be when I grow up, so will you please forgive me?"

Tom bent over to be eye-to-eye with April. He looked directly into her eyes, hesitated for a moment, and then said, "April you were not out of line. But I appreciate your sensitivity and understanding. You will go far in life when you are considerate of others and their feelings." He reached out his hand, she took it, and the two shook on an unspoken agreement.

Once inside again, the three of them sat in the living room munching on fruit and vegetables. There was a large television in the room, but it did not go on. April was glad, it was better for them to talk. And boy, oh boy, did they ever talk.

Tom wanted to know all about Barbara's reunion, her trip, and how she met April. He also wanted to know about April, her family, and all about her. That did not go so well. April only answered direct questions, and vaguely. She was not "best friends" with Tom, and she did not know him that well. He never offered to be her Grandfather either.

That night April went upstairs to her bed. Barbara was ready to tuck her in when April just reached out for her. She hugged her around her neck, and buried her face into her chest. Barbara could feel the moisture from April's tears. "What wrong? Oh, honey, don't cry. Tell Barbara what is wrong." April could only snuggle her face deeper into Barbara chest, and breathe in gulps. She was so sad. Barbara held onto her, rocking her back and forth. Barbara almost began to cry, but held it in. She could only imagine the deep sadness this little girl had leaving her family, and no Mother. She may fool everyone with her knowledge and savvy, but she was only six years old.

Barbara rocked this little girl for almost half an hour. Soon April's grip became less and less. Barbara tucked her into the bed and covered her lightly. She was sure to turn on the night light so if April awakened, she would not be frightened. The she closed the door half way to allow her to go out if she chose.

As Barbara went out, in came their dog Tootsie. She acted like this room was hers, which it definitely was not. Tootsie came in past Barbara's legs, looked at that little bed, hopped right up, circled around twice, and laid down beside April. Tootsie sniffed April, and licked her face.

"Tootsie," Barbara said in hushed tones, "stop that." Tootsie stretched out, and closed her eyes. In her doggy mind, April was for her to take care of. So that was that!

Barbara went out, and sat down in the den. Her husband came in, and asked, "Are you alright?"

"No. No I am not," and Barbara began to release the tears she felt rocking April. "Tom, I know all of our children are grown and gone. I know that. And I know we have eleven grandchildren, and we are close to retirement. But I can't help it. Every fiber in my body is screaming at me, saying that little girl back there has no one. I know it. just as I know my life. She cried herself to sleep. Imagine that! When have you, I, our children, or any of our grandchildren cried themselves to sleep?"

"Honey, you are upset. I see that, but you must think rationally. This little girl is on her way to California to meet her Aunt. For her Aunt to take care of her until her Mother is well again."

"I don't believe it. I just don't," said Barbara. That sweet little girl does not know the Aunt's name or the town she lives in. She cannot remember what the Aunt looks like. That Aunt has never visited them, and they never traveled to California to visit her. It's a madeup story I tell you, and it's killing me. I just can't send her on. I just can't."

"Barbara, listen to yourself," Tom said. "You are not talking rationally."

"I may not be," Barbara said. "But I am a mother, and my gut instincts tell me. It's like an alarm bell going off. I just know that this little girl is on her own. I know it. Everything about her tells me so. And for the life of me, it may kill me to send her on to nowhere, with no one to take care of her."

"Honey, you are tired, and it's getting late. You should sleep on this, and then you can look at the pros and cons in the morning."

Barbara was angry. She did not get angry often, but she knew she was right. Nothing would change her mind, and most certainly not morning. Yes, they were older, fifty-nine and sixty-two respectively. That did not mean they were too old to raise one more child. They certainly had the means. They were not poor in any sense, and this little girl was a humble little thing.

Barbara did not know what to do. She thought, "Well, when I don't know what to do, I do nothing, and usually something turns up." So she got up, and the two of them headed to their room. Barbara threw her robe on a chair and flopped into bed. She turned on her left side away from her husband. Tom saw this and he lay beside her with his arm around her.

"Honey, I love you dearly. All I am asking is that we talk this out. okay? Good night Sweetheart", and soon he was asleep. He was, but not Barbara. She lay there with her mind racing, then she got out of bed, and knelt. She was not sure why she was doing this, but she knew it would give her relief. April was a good example, and Barbara knew she should pray when she least felt like praying. As she did, she felt the burdens lift from her, not all at once but manageable. At *Amen*, she went back into bed. Tom was snoring, As she listened to him, she soon fell asleep.

The next morning, Tootsie was April's constant companion. Wherever April was, Tootsie was too.

April asked if she would be allowed to go swimming in their pool, so Tom put some floats in the water. He asked April if she could indeed swim. "Sure I can," April said. "Can you?" and he laughed at her. He could see why Barbara wanted to keep her. She was such an amiable little girl, pleasant and not troubling.

April swam like a little fish. She even went jumping off the diving board, while Barbara held her breath. "Be careful," she said.

April was not afraid. She backed up on the diving board, ran with all she had, jumping and holding her knees. "Cannonball," she yelled, and splash, she would come up laughing.

Barbara would clap her hands, "Good for you. Wow!" Soon the swimming was over, and April was hungry. "Me too," said Barbara. "But we are not going to eat a lot, because tonight we are getting together with my children. We are having a big picnic at the lake. You'd like that wouldn't you, April?"

"Oh, yes. Yes, I would," April said. "Will there be games to play too?" she asked.

"Oh, I am sure there will be," answered Barbara. "How about later, you help me find some games that would be fun. They are out in the pool house." April just sat there, and grinned excitedly at the thought of a picnic.

The telephone rang, and Tom said he would get it. There was a brief conversation, and soon Tom came out to tell Barbara what it was all about - their sons were at the daughter's home, and they would be heading to the lake within a few hours. They would set up the barbecue and shore fires.

With that, Barbara tapped the top of April's hand. "I'd say we should get the thing all out, and then get our suits and stuff. Okay?"

"YES," said April. And they left to do just that.

The time dragged, at least to April. Barbara was bustling all, around getting things together. Tom sat and read the newspaper. The telephone rang again, and this time Barbara answered it, "Hello. Oh, Hi, Sarah. How are you? Yes, yes, okay. Well, I think we are leaving soon. Hold on a minute. Tom, Sarah and the kids want to know if we are leaving soon?"

Tom said, "Okay." He got up, put his sandals on, and went out to get their van. Barbara finished the call, then she and April began to lug around the stuff they had readied near the door. Tom carried the stuff from the house to the van.

Soon they were in the van heading to the lake. April sat in the back with her window open a little, her hair blew in the breeze. It was much nicer than the bus, and Barbara asked her if she wanted to watch a movie. April was amazed that on the back of the front seat was a box that could show a movie. It was really something to see, but April said she would much rather watch the scenery as they traveled to the lake. April was always looking for horses. When she saw one, she made a sucking sound, as if she were frightened.

When she did it the first time, it caused concern for Tom. "Are you alright?" he asked. He looked in the rear view mirror, and Barb nudged his side laughing. She explained to him April's love and excitement for horses.

There were many beautiful homes. Some were log homes, some were big on stilts, but they were all so different. Many had flowers and shrubs, and some had statues like deer or ducks that looked real.

As they drove along, the landscape began to change. This was a state park, and there were forests with trees of all kinds. As they drove along, the road looked more like sand than ground. The smell became different too. April loved the woods, the smell of pine trees, and the sound the wind made as it traveled through their boughs. The gravel made sounds unfamiliar to her. It was almost like the sound the skid steer on grit made. And on they drove. The air smelled wet and heavy. There was a flock of ducks that had flown over, and April knew they could not be that far from water. After a while April could see a body of water. In the distance there were cars and a big parking lot. Beyond that was the beach and water. She did not see many boats until they came closer. The boats were far off to the right. Most of them were turned upside down, and anchored with chains.

The Picnic at the Lake . . .

The three of them arrived at the lake around noon. They drove into the lake park lane slowly. They looked around for their children or their vehicles. There had to be over a hundred cars, and there were people all over. They drove for ten minutes around to the bottom loop of the lake, and there Barbara saw the vehicles.

They parked at the closest spot possible, so they would not have to carry their things too far. And soon one of their sons came out. As he did he hugged his Dad, and kissed Barbara's cheek.

He saw April, and bent down to her height. He held out his hand saying, "Hi, my name is Luke. You must be April."

"Yes, I am. And it is very nice to meet you too," answered April.

Luke laughed at her, and he helped his parents take some of the items out of the van. "No need to lock it until everything is out. It's okay. Our things were safe, and no one took our stuff," Luke said. So everyone carried things to their picnic spot.

When the others saw Tom and Barbara coming, they all went to help them. Tom said, "We are okay. There is more in the van. Go and get that," and they did. They all worked together like a group of army ants, to and fro. The smaller kids did not help, they stayed at the lake area playing. When finished setting up, Tom and Barbara sat down.

April stood by Barbara's chair when a very pretty woman came up to April. "Hello, April, my name is Sarah. This is my Mother," and she pointed to Barbara.

April said, "Pleased to meet you."

Then Sarah said, "Maybe you would enjoy playing with the kids at the lake area. April looked at Barbara, and she nodded to go by waving her fingers up and out.

So April left to meet Barbara's grandchildren. There were many of them, and it was difficult to get their names right. But they made mud pies and roads, and ran around. They were just having fun untilo they heard their names being called. It was time to eat.

There were hamburgers, hot dogs, potato salad, macaroni salad, tuna salad, so much food that April doubted all of it would be eaten. She would nibble on something, and try another. Then feel full, go to play, and come back. April felt such freedom. It was amazing to do things and never be reprimanded, or yelled at.

The grandchildren were a lot of fun. They were good natured, and laughed a lot. April thoroughly enjoyed being with them all. They went swimming, and caught some crabs along the shoreline which one of the younger kids wanted to keep as pets. There were no pets with any of them. The lake did not permit any pets because of them "going" in the water or on the shoreline. The picnic ended all too soon. Some of the children began feeling sleepy. The air became cooler, so they all decided to pack up and go home.

April went to each one of them to thank them for inviting her, and letting her have fun playing with their children. They were all impressed. Usually their kids came and went, not caring. And they made this comment to their Mother. "I know," said Barbara. "Look, I love you kids, all of you. But I'd keep this little one in a heartbeat, if I could." Some of the kids thought it would be a bad idea since their Mother could get in a lot of trouble if she kept April. "No! I don't think so," said Barbara. "Who in the world would be waiting for their niece, and not provide an address or telephone number? Since she's been with me, I have tried to contact her Aunt in California for hours, early and late California time. There is no one by that name or address. The address is the bus station. I don't believe there is anyone waiting for her. Tom thinks I am crazy. Call it instinct, or call it intuition. This is not a good situation, and it bothers me greatly."

They all hugged their Mother and Dad, and soon they were all on their way back to their homes. April fell asleep in the back of the van. She had played hard, eaten a lot, and could not stay awake. Barbara turned to look at April slumped over onto her left side. Her blonde hair ringlets were bobbing in the wind coming in her window. Her eyes were closed tight, and her eyelids were a light rose to blue color. "Just beautiful," Barbara breathed.

"Excuse me?" said Tom. "Did you say something?"

"Nothing," said Barbara. "I didn't say anything," and they traveled on home.

Saying Goodbye is Never Easy . . .

Spending time with Barbara and Tom was fun, with endless days of shopping, playing, swimming, and eating out. April soon became restless, and at dinner one night at a local restaurant, she asked, "How long before I leave to go to my Aunt's home?"

Barbara was stunned. "Don't you like it here with us, honey?" she asked.

"I do. But my Aunt must be wondering what happened to me, and where I am by now," April replied.

"I agree with April," Tom commented. "I think we should call the bus line in the morning, and secure a ticket so she can continue her route. Don't you agree, Barb?" he asked.

Barbara pushed food around on her plate. Without looking up she said, "I don't know. We can do that, but I just don't know."

April instinctively touched Barbara on her arm. "It's alright. I will be alright. I know that no matter where I go, you will be here. And if I need you, you will come," April said. Barbara's eyes began to fill with tears, and she put her napkin to her nose as if to blow it and wiped her eyes.

The conversation died, and soon they were checking out to go home. There was not one word between Barbara and her husband. She felt as if her heart was breaking, and he did not understand. He did not want to understand. In such little time, this little girl had stolen her heart with her innocence and open love. She sighed out loud.

"Are you tired dear?" Tom asked.

"Yes. I am just tired, I guess" she answered. April was sitting in the back seat watching, not saying anything just relaxing and thinking how good this was, that two people cared for her in a way hers did not or could not.

When they got home, Barbara helped April get ready for bed. "Will you say prayers with me?" April asked. They both knelt by the side of the twin bed where April slept. With heads bowed April prayed. "Dear Father in heaven, please watch over us tonight. Keep us in your care, and see that we get the rest that we need. Watch over those who are sick in their bodies or in their hearts. Bless Momma, my family, and my Aunt in California. That she is not too worried about me, and that I will see her soon. Bless Barbara and Mr. Tom that they will not miss me too much. And that they will be happy together with their families. We love you Father with all our hearts. Amen."

As she stood up, Barbara's eyes were full of tears, and she hugged April firmly. "I am being very selfish you know. I am going to miss you great bunches. You have brought so much happiness to me and into our home. Why, even Tootsie is going to miss you. And there Tootsie was, doing circles on the floor beside April for attention.

"Awe, I am going to miss you too, Tootsie," April said as she bent over to pet the dog. And she kissed her on her long nose.

Barbara gave April a big bear hug rubbing her back, "Okay, Toots, into bed you go," Barbara said, and soon April was asleep.

Barbara went out and checked where her husband was. He was sitting in his chair in the living room reviewing charts, and she knew he hated to be disturbed. So she bustled about in the kitchen - making out a grocery list, running the dishwasher, putting the laundry into the drier, and then . . . "Now what?" She asked herself. Barbara went to the stairway, picking up newspapers, and putting them in a basket in the kitchen. She lined up the shoes, straightened the living room, and walked back and forth several times before she could calm herself down.

Barbara was troubled. She ran scenarios through her head. Each time she was concerned, and began to walk again - to the kitchen, through the living room, up the hallway and back. "I don't know what to do. I don't know how to contact this person. I have tried. God knows I have tried." She sighed and sat down, and opened a magazine. She flipped through page after page, and then closed it. She put it on a stack of others when she noticed a drawing April had made for her.

Barbara almost began to cry again, and she said to herself, "Okay, Barbara, enough is enough. Do what you can do about it, and then trust." So she got out a notepad and began a letter to the illusive Aunt that she had tried to contact sixty-four times in the five days April was with them. She began her letter:

Dear Auntie,

I do not know your name. You are illusive to me, but I trust that you will take guardianship over April, and treasure that responsibility. We have grown to love this little girl as our own. I feel a sense of foreboding sending her on, to continue her journey on the bus. I feel as if there is something wrong, and I only want to protect her. If for any reason you change your mind, and do not want the responsibility of caring for her until her Mother is well, please know that we will come and get her anytime, anyplace. It would be our privilege to care for her until we are notified to return her. The cost is irrelevant.

Please understand, we tried to contact you when we decided to let April take a break from the long bus ride to California, and stay with us for a while. There was no address, only a bus station address. We called that station stop to let them know April's passenger number would be delayed, and resume her trip within five days or a week. But they acted as if they did not know anything. That concerned me to the point of alarm. We were aghast that no one would make preparations for such a little girl, to leave word or a message. We concluded you may work long hours, or may not have a telephone. Maybe it is such a small town that a bus station employee or janitor there may know you personally, or would get the message to you. So with a heavy heart I am sending your niece on to you in California. All I ask is that you kindly respond to my note, so I have peace of mind knowing that April has arrived to her new home in California and she is safe. I cannot say enough how much this little girl means to us. I can't imagine sending her off on her own. She is smart, and can take care of herself. But as a Mother, I could not personally do this. So I have to believe her Mother is very, very ill.

In closing I want you to also know that if you are deprived of finances and cannot properly take care of April, we are willing to help you in that manner. Please do not hesitate to call us. And when she is settled in, I would love to see her again, in her own home, her own setting. That may be a lot to ask, but I pray you will be kind and allow this to me. For you see this little girl has taught me much in the way of faith. So I am trusting that this letter will reach you when April does, and hoping you will kindly respond.

Sincerely,
Barbara Cunningham.
9470 Sailors Way, TN

Barbara folded the note, went into the kitchen, got an envelope, and sealed the letter inside. She went up to where April was sleeping, and put the letter inside her suitcase. On the right side there was a small elastic material to hold something small, it was empty, and the envelope fit right inside without being noticed.

Early the next morning, Barbara called the bus station line number. She was on hold for what seemed like eternity, and she asked her husband to hold the telephone while she went to the bathroom. When she came out, Tom was off of the phone reading the newspaper. "Well, what happened?" Barbara asked.

"I got it. She is to be there at 10:00 am."

"Well thanks a lot. I thought I'd take her out to lunch or something like that, so the trip would not seem so long. I don't know who will take her out for lunch." Barbara snapped.

Barbara went into the kitchen to boil some eggs, and make some sandwiches. She was busy, and did not notice Tom enter. "What's the matter?" he asked.

"The matter? Are you kidding me? Tell me you do not notice or understand how I feel about this little girl," Barbara barked.

"Yes, I see it. But she is not yours," Tom answered.

"I don't believe she is anyone's. And all I wanted was one last day with her. And YOU . . . all you want is for her to be gone."

"No, that's not true," Tom said back. "But I do believe it would be best if she were on her way, and we got back to our lives," and he walked out.

"Back to your lives, back to our lives," Barbara thought. "I love my husband, but no man is going to direct my life. I worked back-breaking jobs so he could finish his residency, and umpteen kids later that I almost raised single-handedly. I am to live his life? No. Nope, that's not going to happen. He has his job, and I will have a life. And that was that!"

Sandwiches were made, and treats packed, along with fruit and some snackable vegetables. Barbara went to get April who was already up and dressed. "Well, Pumpkin. Today is the day," Barbara cheerfully said.

"What do you mean?" April asked.

"Today is the day you leave to go to California. I have already made some sandwiches for you, so you don't have to worry about stopping and getting off. I am not going to be there, and I just want you to be safe," Barbara said.

April hugged Barbara's legs and said, "I love you, Barbara." Barbara almost melted. They went downstairs. They had two hours before they had to leave.

"How about we pack up your clothes, and make sure we have everything. We'll check the drier, and then you and I will take a trip to town before you have to leave," Barbara said.

"Okay," April replied, and she went skipping to get her backpack, suitcase and beloved tiger. Barbara laid out her clothing. She had bought April a number of sets, and hoped they would all fit. "Here are somethings that are a little old. Do you want to keep them?" Barbara asked.

"Yes, I do. They are mine." April said as she put them into her backpack.

"Here darling. Let me roll them before you put them in, that way you can put in more," and Barbara winked at her. Soon they were all packed and ready to go.

Tom asked if Barbara wanted him to go along with her. "No," she said. "I am not upset with you. I understand. I started this little journey with her quite innocently, but now I will end it too. But it's just hard," and Tom held her and kissed her cheek.

He did understand. It was very hard having the last child leave their home. Oh yes, they do visit, and they are good kids. It is just difficult not having them to care for and do things with anymore. "We're old," he chuckled, and he went back to his charts. He did not have to be at work until one o'clock. He wanted to bring home dinner for Barbara. He knew she would not be in any frame of mind to cook.

Barbara and April headed into town, and she stopped at a place called The Sweet Shop. "How about we go in and have a nice ice cream sundae?" Barbara asked April.

April pursed her lips, "No, I'd rather not. I would rather just be with you, maybe a walk or something."

So Barbara got out of the van, walking to April's side, and said, "A walk it is." They saw a small park, and April sat on a swing. Barbara went behind her holding onto the chains on either side. "Hold on. I'm going to push hard," and April laughed and giggled with each push.

As they went they chatted small talk, hand in hand. "Oh, I am going to miss this," Barbara said to herself. Her granddaughter was wild and spoiled, and she could not walk in town with the granddaughter without the girl asking for everything she saw. April was not like that. She was calm, confident, and comfortable on her own. The truth was, Barbara did not choose April, it was the other way around. April could have been with any person on that bus, but it was Barbara she tapped.

They saw a vendor with warm pretzels, and Barbara bought two. "Do you want mustard on yours?" Barbara asked April.

"Oh, yes. Yes I do. I love mustard," April replied.

Barbara looked at her watch often, but this time it was time to head to the bus station. Barbara looked at her small companion and said, "Okay, Kiddo. It's time we head to the bus station."

"Already?" April asked.

"Come on," Barbara said. Into the van they went, and within minutes they arrived at the central bus station. It took Barbara a little time to explain about the week detour in Tennessee, and to resume the ticket to California.

The ticket handler was a young girl who was new at this job. She was confused, and needed help. So then a much older man, who was a supervisor, came to help. He got all the information, and chatted with Barbara. He assured her not to worry, all customers are watched over, no matter if they are five or one hundred and five.

Barbara handed him the money to pay for the difference, and soon she was headed to the benches where April was sitting. Barbara stuffed receipts into her purse. She put a band on April's wrist and a ticket into the pocket of April's sweater. "It's already stamped, and you are good to go," Barbara said. "Will you hand me your tiger?" Barbara asked. April did so willingly. Barbara said, "I know that you keep money in here, and I sewed a zipper instead of just having a hole. I am going to put some money in here in case you need anything. If you get hungry or want a book or a toy, or maybe some shoes. Or . . ."

April touched her arm. "I'll be alright. I appreciate all you did for me. I have to go, even though part of me doesn't want to. But my life is waiting for me in California, and your life is here with Mr. Tom. You know that. Don't you?" Barbara leaned over to hug her. Both of them had tears in their eyes.

April hugged her, and then put her face directly in front of Barbara's, and said, "I love you. Don't you ever forget that. I will never forget you or how kind you were to me, not ever. One day you and I will see each other, and hug each other again as friends. And we will laugh and have fun. I promise."

Barbara had no words. How could someone so young be so mature, so full of faith. She was in awe of this little girls strength and ability to move on in this horrible circumstance she was in.

Barbara hugged her and said in a whisper, "I am going to hold you to that promise. I hope it is true. I want to see you all grown up. Okay?"

April whispered back to her, "I promise you, and I will," and the two of them hugged a long, long hug. Barbara kissed her cheeks and forehead when they heard the announcement for the departure of their bus. They got up, April put her backpack on, tiger under her arm, suitcase in hand, and they headed to the bus. There was already a line of people, and April left Barbara's side to enter the line.

"Tickets, tickets," the porter called. April put down her suitcase for a minute to reach for her ticket in her pocket, and resumed her walk. The porter had to look down instead of in front of him, and he was very patient, "What do we have here?"

"I am going my Aunties' house in California," April answered him.

"You don't say." Taking her ticket he said.

"Oh, but I do say," she mocked him. And he smiled at her patting the top of her head. He then said something to the girl at the bus door, and she repeated it to the driver. This driver was not Ed.

April entered the bus door, and those steps were still very steep for her. A young lady helped her navigate them She said, "Why don't you sit right there, behind the driver? You will have a better view on your trip."

"I know," said April. "That's always my seat." She settled in, and did not notice Barbara standing to the side of the bus with tears running down her cheeks. Barbara could barely breathe.

Everyone was soon on the bus, and April saw the driver. He was a very young man, who was dressed very snappy. He was coming up the steps, and April asked him, "What will be our first stop?"

"First stop, already? We haven't even started," and he laughed. He said, "This is going to be a long haul. We will not be stopping until we reach the far side of Oklahoma, and then we might stop in either Texas or New Mexico."

"Wow," April thought to herself excitedly. Cowboys and cowgirls just like she hoped to be. She knew that she was part Native American from what her Mother told her. She never wanted to be a cowgirl to chase Indians. She wanted everyone to be kind to each other, but she loved rodeos. She went once with her Grandpa, it was fine. She loved the bull riding and the calf roping. She sat in her seat electrified with excitement while her Grandpa laughed.

On to Texas

As the bus began to pull out, Barbara was waving goodbye with a hankie hoping to catch April's attention. April stood up looking for Barbara, and began to wave back. "You have to sit down," the driver said.

April did, very quickly. And she waved and blew kisses, until she could not see Barbara anymore. April realized very quickly this bus driver was going to be much stricter than Ed was. So she decided to sit in her seat and "keep her trap shut," as her brother's used to say. She had all she needed. She had sandwiches and juices, so she had no need to talk to this snappy bus driver. They certainly had gotten started very wrong.

On the route the bus driver was constantly changing the radio stations. It was quite annoying, and he played the music way to loudly. Riders on the bus soon began to complain, and much to the driver's chagrin, so he played the radio very softly. So that it was difficult to know what song was playing.

April did not care. He reminded her of a spoiled child, cranky, and wanting what he wanted no matter what others wanted. She knew some kids her age that were like that. They were not her friends. They acted like they were better than she was. She remembered a time when her Mother made it clear she was just as good as anyone.

It was after school, riding on the bus. She and two other of her friends were talking about trying out for knee high cheerleading. They were excited, talking in turns, when an older girl came through the aisle, and said to them, "You girls are farmers. You are not ever going to be cheerleaders. You are farmers, and that is all you will ever be." What a blow!

April got off the bus at her stop, and walked the long dirt lane to her home. She must have looked very sad, and most likely was pouting, as her Mother said, "Keep your lip like that, and a bird will poop on it." April said nothing.

"What's the matter?" her Momma said. April told her what the older girl had said to them, and she should know because she was older. When April finished, her Momma said, "Come here," with her arm lifted as if to comfort her. That's when her Momma pulled her over her lap, and began to give April a spanking. When she spanked, Momma said a word and hit. You would want her to either talk fast, or hit every third word or so. "Don't you ever come home saying that you are not as good as anyone else." She stood April up in front of her, and shook April so hard her teeth rattled. "Do you understand me?" Momma said. "If someone has a quarter and you have a quarter, it is the same thing, April. You are as good as anyone else. If you are a farm girl and they are a nurse's daughter, you both have opportunities and choices to make, to make your own life. Momma then took April's face in her hands and said, "God created us all. We all have been created equal, meaning we all have the same choices to make and examples to live. Do you understand?"

April said, "Yes." Never, ever again would she say she could not do something. If she could not hit a ball, April never said she couldn't. She did it. She learned to push herself, to do everything well - as well as she could.

April felt a little sorry for the bus driver. He was not a kid. Well . . . maybe he was more like a kid with adult responsibilities, like a job. Well, who knows what else. April thought that before too long the driver would talk to her nicely. No one likes to be alone if they don't have to be.

And she was right. Soon the driver said to her, "How old are you?"

April answered back, "How old are you?"

The bus driver laughed, and said, "I am thirty-two years young. So how old are you?" And he had a huge smile on his face.

"I am six," April replied.

Then the bus driver said, "Six, wow! You have so much to go through yet in life. Man I remember six, playing with my brothers, going swimming, playing in the yard. Don't you do stuff like that?" he asked.

"I did, but now I am going to my Auntie's home in California. I don't know if she has kids or not." April said. And then she said, "What is your name. We are having a conversation about our lives, and I don't know your name."

"You are right," the bus driver said. "My name is John, everyone calls me Johnnie." That name would be easy for April to remember. She used to tease her brother calling him Johnnie, knowing he did not like to be called that. He preferred to be called John. April soon learned she was wrong about Johnnie. He was a very likeable man, jumpy almost nervous, but nevertheless a happy soul. He liked to crack jokes, "Hey, Toots. What is red and white and black all over?" he would ask.

"I don't know," April said.

Johnnie would laugh and say, "Gotcha. It's a skunk with diaper rash. Ha ha!" Johnnie was just happy and very silly, but he took his job very seriously. He did not like when passengers would leave their seats to walk up front to ask him questions. Johnnie would see them coming and yell, "Sit down, sit down. If you want to ask me something, you either raise your hand or shout it out. Do not leave your seat, and come up front. It is too distracting to your driver."

April was all for good behavior. If you listened and obeyed, you did not get in trouble - unlike her home life. When she was good, she still was picked on. So this situation on the bus seemed just fine to her.

As they drove along, April began to get sleepy. She thought she should go to the bathroom before she got too sleepy and nod off to sleep. So she hopped off of her seat and went slowly, with her hands on the sides of the seats to guide her to the back of the bus. People were talking or reading. Some had music they were listening to on their plastic boxes on their laps. Some were sleeping. Others were eating, and dropping food onto the bus floor. Some were trying to style their hair, and a psst of hairspray got April on her face. She coughed. "Sorry hon, gotta get my hair standing up," the woman said. April finally got to the horrid bathroom, turned the knob and went inside. It was not too bad this time. She went, then washed her hands and the hair spray from her face.

April wiped her hands on a fresh paper towel that she was able to reach from the dispenser, then she turned the knob to open the door. She hit a woman in the leg. "I am sorry, Ma'am," April quickly said.

"Well, you should be. Watch what you are doing. This bus aisle is small. You are not at home," the woman angrily said. April darted under the woman's arm, and went to her seat.

April sat there wondering what that was all about. "So you met Mrs. Battle Axe have you?" Johnnie teased. "I see her on the bus from time to time. She is all talk, a lot of huff, but she can be a really nice person, so don't take what she says too seriously," Johnnie said.

April slunk back into her seat. Using her tiger as her pillow, she began to nod off. She felt something covering her. It was Johnnie putting his jacket on her legs for warmth, using his one arm backwards. April pulled the jacket over her, and soon she was asleep. It sure was nice being around kind, caring people.

On and on and on they drove. April was unaware that they had traveled across most of Oklahoma. She could hear the engine of the bus whine, shift its gears as it went up hills or fast on straight stretches. It was easy to tune it out. It was so routine, she was used to it. April sat up at one point, and said, "Where are we now?"

"Almost to the end of Okiehomie," Johnnie said.

"Did we go past Oklahoma?" April asked almost alarmed.

"No we still have a ways to go. Did you want to stop there?" Johnnie asked.

"Yes. Yes I did. I hoped we would see cowboys and horses and stuff," April said.

"It's not like that anymore, Toots. Oklahoma is a city, all civilized with big businesses and high rise buildings. The countryside of Oklahoma is shrinking fast." That made April sad. She wanted to meet cowboys so much, so she sat down and just thought. "I smell smoke" Johnnie said, looking directly at her, "Whatcha thinking about?"

"Oh, not much. Just that I won't get to see any cowboys or horses," April said.

"Oh, don't get me wrong," Johnnie said. "There are cowboys and horses in Oklahoma, but not in the city. And that is where we are heading, to another bus stop."

They drove on, and April slipped in and out of sleep. Daylight was beginning to show along the skyline, and the sun was peeking through. "It's still early there cupcake. Why not try to sleep a little more before we stop?" Johnnie asked her.

"Well, I am usually up early," April answered him.

"Why's that?" he said.

"I grew up on a dairy farm, and we were always up very early," she answered him.

"A dairy farm!" Johnnie proclaimed. "Wow, that is a tough job, long days, and every day. Not for me," and he shook his head. "So why then are you heading to California?" Johnnie asked her.

"I am going to my Aunt's home, and be with her for a while. That's all I know," April answered him. Soon they arrived at the bus terminal. Johnnie jumped up, and used his arms to slide down the steps, not stepping on any of them.

"Hey! What's up," he hollered to someone, and soon he was lost in the big crowd. People began to get off of the bus. April stayed in her seat. Since she did not know what to do, she stayed put. Soon Johnnie was at her side, "Hey, Toots. Aren't you getting off to stretch your legs, and get a bite to eat?"

"I don't think I will," April said. "I don't want to get lost."

"You won't get lost with me," Johnnie said, and he reached his hand out to her. April did not take his hand.

"Nope." she said. "I don't want to. I will stay here until it is time to go again."

"Are you sure?" he asked her. April just nodded her head yes.

Johnnie hollered to a person, and then disappeared into the crowd again. Soon he came back, and he had a pastry of some kind with him. "Want this?" he said to her.

"What is it?" April asked.

"Why this is a pasty, a delicious crust with all sorts of vegetables inside. Let me tell you, this is soooo delicious, Button. You are missing out." April reluctantly stood up.

She looked at Johnnie, and making a fist, shook it at him. The she said, "I will go with you, but you better not lose me, or else." And April firmly set her jaw. Johnnie tried his best not to laugh. He did not even crack a smile. He just looked at her, saluted, and held out his hand. This time April put her tiny hand in his, and followed him down the steps into the crowd.

They went to a place where the pastys were being made. Another man walked up to Johnnie, and asked, "Who's your girlfriend Johno?"

"Well my friend, let me introduce you to Princess April. Mind you to behave, or she will connect her right fist with the left side of your jaw, and lay you out."

"You don't say?" his friend said.

"Hello," he said, and held out his hand to April for a hand shake.

"My name is Fred. I am the supervisor of the chaos here. And I keep the goofy drivers in line." April smiled at Fred. He had the brightest red hair she had ever seen, and the deepest blue eyes ever! April liked Fred instantly. Without any hesitation, she went over to Fred and hugged his legs.

"Whoa there," Johnnie said. "I thought you were my main squeeze, Toots."

Fred quickly picked up the conversation. "So April, what can I do for you? Would you like to accompany me for a bite to eat, and get away from the smelly trash that is making such a stinky smell?"

"Hey, hey," Johnnie said. "Stop trying to take my squeeze away from me. She is my date. I had to do a bit of work to convince her to come with me. Didn't I, Sweetie?" he asked as he looked at April. April was having such a fun time being the center of attention.

She looked at Johnnie, and said, "Yes, you did, but a girl has to take advantage of situations when she can." And both men laughed as they placed their orders.

They bought April a cheese and vegetable cheesesteak. April's tummy growled. She was indeed hungry, and she was very glad she had gotten off the bus. She sat with Fred who had a plate of pierogies and fried vegetables. Johnnie soon joined them with three cups of soda. He sat beside April, giving her a medium sized cup and a straw. "Thank you both so very much. I can pay for my own food. I do have money," she said.

"Well dear, we would much rather sit with you, and enjoy your company. There is something to be said when a female is happy and comfortable with the men in her life. Alas, that has escaped me for a long time," Fred said.

Johnnie quickly added. "If you took a shower every day, your chances would improve." Then Fred threw his napkin at Johnnie.

"Are you going to eat that?" April said, pointing to the pierogies on Fred's plate.

"Do you want these dear? Well then, help yourself," Fred smiled at her.

"A woman who knows what she wants, and not afraid to say so. Imagine that?" Fred said.

"Yeah, and she's all of six years old," Johnnie said. They both rolled their eyes, and laughed.

"Let's both hope she never changes, and goes for life with all the gusto she has," Fred said. "Yeah. And may she become the boss of our company, and keep all of us on our toes," and they laughed again.

Soon a bell rang, and both men stood up. "You can take that with you sweetheart."

"Here. Let Fred wrap that up for you." He did, and handed the bundle to April as she carried her drink.

Johnnie said, "I'll put you on the bus. Then I need to round everyone up, and get my departing time."

April went to Fred, took his hand, and kissed the back of it. "Thank you so very much for being kind to me, and sharing your food. You're a very nice man, and I like you."

Fred rolled his eyes as if in agony. "Why can't I find a young, beautiful 25- or 30-year-old woman with such a good attitude and gratitude?" and he was off.

As they went to their bus and entered, there were kids digging into April's backpack. Her clothing was all over, as well as the things in her suitcase, and her tiger was on the floor. April went into a flurry of anger. She grabbed the boy, and pushed him backwards. And the girl she pushed into the seat on the other side.

"You thieves!" she screamed at them. "It is not your stuff. You should never take things that are not yours."

"Cupcake, Toots, come on. Stop that. I'll take care of this." Johnnie put both of the older kids in one seat, and began grilling them. April began to put her things that were strewn and tossed back into her backpack and suitcase. She picked up her tiger. She saw his bottom was dirty and wet, and she began to cry. She was so mad!

She walked over to the older kids, and using the palm of her hand, she popped them in the forehead. Their heads went backwards. She called them dirty thieves and scumbags. She kicked the boy, and hissed at him.

Johnnie laughed inwardly and tried his best to keep a straight face. This little six year old put the two fourteen year olds in their place. She sure was a tiger when provoked. Johnnie said, "If you ever do this again, I am going to put her on the bus with you alone. And what happens, happens." Their eyes flew open wide.

Soon a woman entered the bus, and spoke another language to the two in the seat behind Johnnie. Johnnie motioned for her to sit behind the kids. They had a flurry of indistinguishable language, then crying and screaming.

Johnnie had enough! He told the woman what her two darlings had done. Then he told her that unless she paid for the damage right here and now, he would be forced to file a formal complaint. She and the kids would be removed from the bus, and there would be criminal charges filed. He quoted an amount she would have to pay. She quickly opened her purse, pulled out the amount, and pushed it into Johnny's hand. Then she grabbed the girl and boy by the hair, and pulled them out of the bus. She pushed them in front of her, and they soon disappeared into the crowd.

Johnnie helped April put her things away. He used his finger to wipe away the tears on her cheeks, and he said, "Hey, come on now. Big girls don't cry."

April looked at him with her heart melting and eyes filled with tears. She said, "Oh, yes they do, but not many people get to see them when they do."

Johnny took her tiger, and using wet wipes he kept with him, he scrubbed the white and yellow orange fur clean. He then took the tiger to her, and said, "Put him by the heater so he can dry, then brush the fur. Then he will be as good as new."

April's heart was touched, and she said, "Thank you Johnnie. I don't know why people have to be so mean and greedy. They have a Mother with them. I don't. They have money, and are not poor. What's wrong with them that they can't be happy with what they have? Why do they take from others when they know it is not theirs?"

"I don't know, Cupcake. If we could figure that out, we could change the world, you and I." And with that, he took the microphone off of the cradle and began to call the passengers back on the bus.

With the announcement made, slowly the passengers began to board the bus. April saw, from the corner of her eye, the two kids and their Mother board. They did not look at her - their eyes were front and center.

Soon everyone was on the bus. Johnnie took the mic out again, and said, "We are leaving in five minutes. Make yourselves comfortable for another long haul. Our next stop will be Texas." He flipped off the mic, put it back in the cradle, and stretched. Then he sat down.

Soon the engine of the bus started, and the air conditioner began. "Hey, want to watch a movie?" He asked April. "Pick one out, and I'll play it for the bus," Johnnie said.

April looked at the movies kept in a box by Johnnie's seat. "I don't know movies, I would not know what one people would like," April said.

"Just pick one, and they will watch it," Johnnie said. So she rifled in the box, and found one that looked western. There was a picture of an older cowboy with a patch on his eye, and a young girl with short dark hair. She had a hat on, and was sitting on a pony.

She handed it to Johnnie. "Ah, this is a good one. Ever see it before?" he asked her.

April said, "No."

It was a very good movie. It had a lot of action and horse riding. April liked the girl in the movie. She was young, but was determined to find the man who had killed her father. She wanted to bring him to justice. As the movie ended they were in full daylight - it was a beautiful sunny day. Johnnie had on sunglasses that April thought made him looked like a movie star.

On and on they drove. There is little to do on a bus, you must entertain yourself. So April pulled out her suitcase and some paper, and began to draw. She decided to draw her latest friends, Fred and Johnnie. That took her quite a while to draw. When she was finished, she reached forward to hand the picture to Johnnie. "What's this?" Johnnie asked.

"It's a picture of you and your friend Fred," April said.

Johnnie said, "What a masterpiece! I am going to save it. And when I see Fred again, I am going to tease him with it. I will tell him I have a gift from you, and he did not get one." With that April quickly thought she should make another for Fred. Then Johnnie said "Fred is more than a friend, he is my cousin. We spend a lot of time together when we are not working. He loves to fly fish, and so do I. We often take our four-wheelers to the farm, and fly fish in the streams."

That satisfied April that one picture was enough. She was very glad Johnnie and Fred were not only friends, but cousins. April knew she had cousins, but did not know where they lived, or much about them. They lived far away, and as she thought about it, she wondered why her family did not send her to her cousin's home. Well, it makes no sense to wonder about something that never happened. I might as well just deal with what I have, and that's that.

On their bus raced. Johnnie did exceed the speed limit. April could see the speed dial, and often the arrow pointed to eighty or eighty-five. But she felt perfectly safe, Johnnie really concentrated on the road as they whizzed along.

April began to feel restless, so she watched out of her window. As they drove along, she was able to see ranches with white board rails. She perked up in her seat, and watched with pure intent on seeing horses. She saw longhorn cattle, sometimes goats and sometimes sheep, but only occasionally horses. When there were, she'd turn her head backwards to see the horses as long as she could. The people in the seats behind her would smile and wave at her. April would sometimes wave back, then turn, and sit forward in her seat. She wished and wished to see lots of horses.

"What are you looking for, Toots?" Johnnie asked. "Are you looking for cowboys?"

"No, I am looking for horses. I am always looking for horses," she answered.

"Well, they are all round us, but not so many along the main highways that we are travelling. You see over there, that way," and he pointed to a small rise of a hill. "Back that way is a big ranch. I used to stop there to see a girl I knew. There were hundreds of horses there, but again, not along the main highway." April was both happy and sad. She was happy there were still many horses in the west, but sad that she could not see them along the way their bus was going.

The hours went by, from lunchtime to dinnertime. April had the last of the lunches of fruit and vegetables that Barbara had sent along with her. She was down to the last bunch of grapes when she noticed Johnnie looking at her from his mirror. "Do you want my grapes?" she asked him.

"I thought you'd never ask me, Toots. I love grapes." Johnnie grinned and laughed. April handed her Ziploc bag with grapes inside to him, and he winked at her saying, "Thank you."

"You're welcome," April answered.

"Wow, these grapes are sweet. As sweet as you are," and April blushed.

"Oh, you are such a tease," she said to him. And Johnnie laughed at her.

By lunchtime, the passengers on the bus were beginning to grumble that they wanted to stop. Johnnie reached up for the mic, and announced, "Folks, settle down. We are driving a little further to get you to one of the best home-cooked dinners around. It's a little out of the way, but you will all be glad when we get there," and hung up his mic. "Geez, those adults complain more than you do, April. What's up with that?"

April answered him, "Maybe they did not go to kindergarten."

"What do you mean by that?" Johnnie asked her.

"They do not know how to wait or take turns," April replied, and again Johnnie laughed.

"Toots, you're alright. I hope one day when I am married. Oh, God. Well, if and when that happens. I hope to have a little girl with hutzpah just like you - it would be good."

Soon they were slowing down to a ramp to exit the highway. All of the passengers began to get ready to exit the bus. Some were combing their hair, fixing their makeup, or straightening their clothes. Some were searching in their bags or purses, and it was interesting to watch them.

Johnnie watched carefully as he weaved in and out of traffic. He put on his turn signal to get over into another lane. "Puss bucket! He drove right in front of me, cutting me off. Dang it all anyway." Soon he was turning into the parking lot of a Texas restaurant.

As the bus brakes screeched to a stop, everyone began to stand up. Johnnie again reached for his mic. "Listen up people. Sit down. Sit down. Listen up!!!! We are stopping here for one-and-one-half hours. Get it? One-and-one-half! By that time I expect everyone to be out here at the bus. Do you all know the difference between a tourist and a hitchhiker? Five minutes! I am NOT going to go around searching for you. If you are not here, it is likely you will be left behind. Got that?" He opened the door, and out they filed. April wanted to get off, but waited until everyone had passed her. She took money out of the zip compartment of her tiger. It was a ten dollar bill, and she thought, "Thank you, Barbara." She hopped up to go out. Johnnie was standing at the door, and said, "You sure like a man to wait long enough for you, doncha?" April smiled, and showed him the ten dollar bill.

"Is this enough money to eat here?" she asked.

"No, put that away. Tell you what. I will treat you this time, and next time you treat me. Okay?"

"Okay," April said.

In they went. This was not a fancy place, but it felt homey. There were nice curtains on the windows, clean carpeting, and waitresses going to and fro through the building. There was a huge display case of cakes and pies. Some were the biggest cakes April had ever seen. Johnnie pulled her along by the sleeve. He was going so fast, she could not see everything. Suddenly she stopped. Johnnie let go and stopped too. "What's up, Toots?" he said.

April pointed up to the wall and said, "Look!" And there, up on the far wall, was the biggest fish tank she had ever seen.

"Pretty impressive? Isn't it?" Johnnie asked. "Come on. We will get a table close to the tank. Then you can get close, and watch them." And they did.

Their table was a booth. It sat right along the back side wall of the restaurant, and April stood on the seat to watch all the activity in the fish tank. Suddenly a Grouper came toward her, and opened its mouth as if to eat her finger. So she pulled her hand away fast. Johnnie laughed at her, "He can't get you on this side. Don't be afraid." April held her finger still for the second pass of the Grouper. He kept trying and trying to get her finger, and could not.

"He is so silly," April said.

"Okay, Toots. Sit down, and decide what you want to eat," Johnnie said to her.

April did, but since she could not read the menu. She looked for pictures, but there were none. "What are you getting, Johnnie?" she asked.

"Me? Well, I think I am going to have the haddock with a salad and maybe a potato or French fries. What are you having?" he asked her.

April said, "I don't know. I can't read the menu."

Johnnie did not realize because she was so mature. But she WAS only six, and could not read the slanted, italicized words. "Okay. What do you like to eat? Let's start there," he said.

April answered, "I like mashed potatoes, cheese noodles, meatloaf, chicken legs, and she went on and on. Johnnie could not help but realize that this little girl knew about good food. She had to have come from a home where good meals were provided. "How about I order meatloaf with mashed potatoes and a vegetable of green beans for you?" he said.

"Oh, that sounds so good," April said with a big smile in the sheer anticipation of a good meal.

Their food was served very quickly. "Boy, that was fast," April said.

"Yeah. They are fast in here. That is one reason I like it here - no dawdling." April and her companion dug into their meal, and ate with little talking.

April could not help but notice that the girl who brought their food was staring at them. Then she would turn to her co-workers, talk, and they would all laugh.

April got Johnnie's attention. "That girl likes you," she said.

"Who does?" Johnnie asked turning around quickly. Their eyes met, and she turned around blushing. "By golly, Miss April, you sure have an eye. Keep eating, and wait here for me," he said. Johnnie got up and out of his seat, and headed towards the young waitress. He went to talk to her, and she blushed. He was with her for a few minutes, wrote something down on a napkin, gave it to her, and then returned to his seat. April just looked at him. "What?" he said with a sly smile.

"If you play games of catch, sooner or later you're going to be caught," April said.

"You're a little minx. Aren't you?" Johnnie said laughing.

"No. I am not, but I have older brothers who teased girls too."

"It's nothing serious. I just want to meet her, and go out on a date. I gave her my phone number, and she gave me hers," he said. April nodded it was good. He was single, old enough to go out on dates, and meet a nice companion. Secretly inside April hoped that soon he would find someone. She had been so wrong about Johnnie in the beginning when they first met. He really was a nice guy.

April waited at the register while Johnnie was back talking to the pretty waitress. Soon he came to the register, flashing out his billfold. He payed for their dinners, and left a twenty dollar tip for his waitress, that pretty girl he gave his telephone number to. What a sly dog, April thought. You get more flies with honey than you do with vinegar - that is what her Momma used to say.

Back on the bus, the passengers settled in for another long, very long ride. When everyone was on, true to his word, Johnnie did not go looking for anyone. "They need to be responsible for themselves," he said, and April could not agree more. Johnnie picked up the mic. "Now that everyone is on the bus, we are leaving, and heading out for New Mexico. Once there we will stop overnight. There has been a little trouble, and we want everyone safe. So for now don't worry about a thing, just hang tight, enjoy the ride, and in a few hours we will be in New Mexico. "Hey, it's not so bad. Maybe you might want to go shopping for a few trinkets or gifts," and he put the mic back into its place.

"Are you ready to rock and roll?" he asked April ruffling her hair.

"Aye yie. Let it rip, Captain," April replied saluting him. He laughed, settling into his seat and strapping in. He started the engine, and soon they were barreling their way towards New Mexico. And then what? April did not know. It was all a mystery. She did not know where she was going, or with whom. It was all a blank page.

The trip was interesting. There were different trees than she had ever seen before. Johnnie told her they were cactus. The cactus looked like a funny man with one leg and many arms up towards the sky, each arm had big prickly things on them. April was sure she did not want to touch them, but they were so neat looking. Some had beautiful, colorful flowers on them. She knew her Momma would have liked to have seen them too. There were many dark-skinned people. Johnnie said they were Mexicans, very hard workers. They were all around. Some had businesses, and some worked in fields. "They are like us," he said. We all bleed red. We all have pain, hunger, need shelter, and care." April understood his words, and never forgot them.

As the bus went on its way, there were many, many things that were very different from the world which April had come from. Here it was hot, and it never snowed. April knew she would miss the snow.

Back home when it snowed, she and her two brothers would go out, and get their sleds. They would pull them up the hills, and it was very difficult considering all the clothing they had on. They usually wore pants and a sweat shirt, then coveralls, boots, a hat, and mittens. So much that you would wobble when you walked. Once they pulled a car hood way up a hillside so they could go sledding. They had previously stuffed the car's hood all along the edges with burlap bags. They did not want to be cut or hurt on the edges.

They would count 1, 2, 3 . . . and then they would jump as fast as they could onto the car hood. Three kids in a small circle, and that car hood would slide down that hill fast - turning left, then right, sometimes making a complete circle. Often she got thrown off, but it was so much fun to scream at the top of your lungs. When she did get thrown off, she laid there in the snow laughing. Whoever made it to the bottom of the hill, had to drag it up part way by themselves. It was a hard job to pull that heavy hood, but so much fun to slide back down.

They had Flexible Flier sleds. They were fun to go downhill, but only two at most could fit on one. Usually Tim would lie down, and April would lie on top of him. She held on as best as she could. They would come flying down the pine tree hill, and would be air born across the hillside that came to their barn. It was so scary, and so much fun.

They would get wet. Their boots filled with snow, and their mittens and gloves would be soaked. Then they would go in the house, and dry off with a hot cup of cocoa. Her Momma made the recipe. She never bought the store's hot chocolate.

This was Momma's hot chocolate recipe. She mixed it in a big silver bowl, and then stored it in a big container.

1 pound of dry milk.
1 22-ounce container of coffee creamer
1 and ½ containers of Nestle chocolate
1 bag of confectionary sugar, the white powdery sugar
1 bag of mini marshmallows

This recipe was mixed every winter, and it lasted almost all winter long. We used four or five heaping teaspoons in a cup of hot water, it was delicious.

Yes, it was very pretty here in Texas. And it was much warmer here than when April left home, but she would miss wintertime on the east coast. The snow would look so pretty. It made everything white, and look so clean. Winter made everyone slow down, come inside, and get warm.

Often friends or neighbors would come to visit on their farm in the wintertime. Momma always had cake or pie on hand with a cup of hot cocoa. And wintertime was a time for Momma to make delicious soups and warm pot roasts. It was so amazing to go in the house after school, and smell what was for dinner.

Wintertime was also the time when Momma made her famous nut rolls. For many months they would pick up black walnuts and walnuts from their trees. They would spend many hours cracking the shells, and picking out the nuts. Then placed them in jars to be sealed for later use.

Momma would make nearly a hundred nut rolls, and sell them. Many times people came to our home to buy them, or we took them with us to school or to the neighbors. Once a man offered Momma a lot of money for her recipe, and she refused. It was her Mother's recipe, and over a hundred years old.

Many people would say they have a good recipe, and Momma would give them a sample. Their faces would change and they would say, "My recipe, or so-and-so's recipe is good, but not as good as yours. Then they would buy several.

They had a rich nutty taste, and were soft and delicious. It was a home staple for as long as she could remember. April might remember how to make it, if she had help. Maybe when she was older, then she would try. Or, maybe Momma would help her.

From the bus April could see different types of animals. She did not know the names of some of them. Some dogs were tiny and snappy. And she saw cattle that had horns that were so long. Johnnie told April those were longhorn cattle. It was all so exciting and new to April.

Soon the bus stopped in Texas, and the news was quite upsetting to some of the passengers. Johnnie pulled down the mic, "Okay, people. We have a problem. Our bus needs to be down for service. There is engine trouble. As much as I would love to just switch to another bus, that is not going to happen until tomorrow about noon. So that said, the bus line is offering you a voucher to stay at a hotel if you chose, and report back to this terminal by 10:30 tomorrow morning. I am sure it will all come together. Do not. I repeat. Do not go to a fancy upscale hotel, or casino and expect the bus line to pay for it. The vouchers are worth fifty dollars. There are many places here in this area and around town that are safe. You can rent a room overnight. If you want help, the staff inside will help you. So okay. Have a nice evening, and nice night. See you all tomorrow at 10:30 a.m. sharp." He clicked off his mic, and said, "Let's you and me boogie out of here. I have a surprise for you."

April was a bit reluctant. She did not know what to do with her belongings. She put on her backpack, held her suitcase and tiger, and stepped down the big steps out of the bus. Johnnie was there talking to a friend, and they high-fived each other. Then Johnnie took her backpack and hand, and they started to run. At times he was almost swinging her along. She began to laugh because it was fun. They reached a parking lot, and Johnnie looked around. Then he said, "There it is. Come on," and he went to a 1966 Ford Mustang. He was so excited. "This is my friend's car, and he is letting us use it until tomorrow morning. He knows me pretty well, so it's cool." He started the engine and it purred. He laughed, shifted pushing in the clutch, and away they sped.

They went out and around the corner of the terminal like lightening. The owner was yelling, "Hey, hey hey!Take it easy. Will ya?" Away they went. Johnny sped up until he was driving sixty-five mph in a thirty-five mph stretch. He was like flying, and glad to be out of that bus. April was not afraid. She did hang onto the armrest as they went flying down the highway.

"Aren't you afraid of being stopped by a police man?" she asked.

"Nah. They are not out now. This is not their stretch. They are mainly on the main routes, nabbing out-of-state drivers for big bucks." he said.

They drove for a while, and then Johnnie started looking left and right. "It's here somewhere," he said. Soon he stopped at a store, well sort of like a store, but it had all sorts of western clothing.

"Do people wear this clothing all the time down here in Texas?" she asked.

"A lot of them do. But you and I have a date, so pick out some duds, and we are out of here," he said in a rush. He asked the clerk if he could use the telephone which she said was alright if it was a local call. He assured her it was. While he was on the phone chatting, the woman helped April pick out an outfit, suitable for their "date".

The sales clerk and April chose a red, white, and blue blouse, a pair of blue jeans, and cowboy boots that were white and red. And last of all a hat. It was white with a red band and a purple plume feather in the band. When Johnnie saw her dressed up, he whistled. "Whit Whew," it went. He paid the woman, and they were out again in a hurry. Johnnie had on black pants, a black shirt with a blue bolo tie. He had a black hat and black boots.

"Are we going to a funeral? If we are, I surely have the wrong clothes," April worriedly said.

Johnnie laughed at her, "Nope. We are going somewhere you are going to love, love, love." And that was all he said.

Before too long they came to a big circus looking building. There were horse trailers all around, horses walking past them, lots of cowgirls that Johnnie could not take his eyes off of, and lots of cowboys. "Where are we" April asked excitedly.

"We, daring girl, are at a rodeo," Johnnie proudly said.

April was thrilled and hollered, "Yipee." Soon he parked the car, and made sure it was not near anything that could cause a scratch. He locked the car doors, and they headed into the rodeo.

At the entryway, Johnnie met a friend who handed him a handful of tickets. "Awe, dude. I only need two tickets, one child for her and one for me," Johnnie said.

"Glad to help you out, cousin. Who is your pretty girlfriend?" the man asked.

"This is April. She is NUTS about horses and cowboys," Johnny answered. "She is always talking about horses, drawing them, or talking about how she had horses and rode. And I believe her. She knows things about horses that I could not imagine. So that's why we are here. It was my surprise to her, and I sure hoped she would have a good time," Johnny said beaming. Looking around he saw many cowgirls scantily dressed, and added, "I think I will too."

The man knelt down to April's height and held out his hand. The rawhide strips of his shirt were dangling down from it. He was dark skinned, and he was a real cowboy. "My name is Travis, and I ride bulls for a living," he said.

April's eyes grew wide, and she asked, "Really?"

"Yes, really," Travis said. "A few more bumps and broken bones may wake me up one of these days and I'll quit. But for now, I am in it one hundred percent. Now you watch for me, okay? I want to hear you cheer for me when I am done, and I hope I make eight. Okay, I have to go. I will look for you when you are inside," and then Travis was gone.

"Oh, I can't believe it," April excitedly said. "I met a real cowboy."

"Oh, you will meet more than one here. My cousin is a regular here, and has a lot of friends who rope and ride." In they went, and April could not help but constantly look all around. They found a seat, a box seat near the arena floor.

They were higher than the animals, but not more than five feet. These were the "most excellent seats" as Johnnie said.

There was calf roping, bulldogging cattle, bronc riding, and bull riding. April could not get enough. At one point she leaned so far over, Johnnie had to pull her back before she went too far forward, and would have fallen into the arena. At intermission time, there were clowns doing funny things. Then there were cowgirls and cowboys on horses asking if anyone who could ride, wanted to ride. Johnnie whistled, a cowgirl came over to where they were, and she asked him to come down.

"Oh, not me. It's her," and he pointed to April.

"Do you know how to ride?" the pretty cowgirl asked.

"And how!" April said as she went scrambling over the side and slid down into the arena. The cowgirl just laughed at her.

"My, you are anxious. Aren't you? Would you like me to help you get on?" she asked. April was already climbing up on the horse on her own. "How about I lead the horse for you around the arena? Would you like me to do that for you?" she asked looking at April.

"Well, cowgirl lady, I would really like to do it on my own. If you don't mind. I mean this is your horse and all, but I am not afraid. I really want to ride by myself. I know how," April excitedly said.

"Okay, then. Off you go," the cowgirl said, and she let go of the bridle. Soon April had the horse walking all around the arena. Some of the volunteers who wanted to ride were older, but were not so good. Some were good, but did not want to ride for long. April did not want to get out of that saddle.

The announcer said, "We have one rider out there that is on her own. Let's see how she does," and he called out to April, "You with the white hat, canter your horse." April made a kissing sound, and kicked the horse as hard as she could. And soon they were cantering all around the arena.

Her hat bounced back, and thankfully was held in place by the string. She was smiling from ear to ear, having the time of her life. "Stop and walk your horse," the announcer said.

April pulled hard back, and the horse stopped so fast he did a rollback. April leaned forward and held onto the saddle horn. People began to clap. "Now trot your horse. Can you do a figure eight?" April did just as he asked, and the people in the stands clapped again. "Folks, it seems we have a rider here. I have to ask. Is this a trick by one of our cowgirls?" the announcer asked. The cowgirl who lent her horse to April, put her arms in the air as if she did not know what was going on either.

Soon that cowgirl was walking up to April, and asked her, "Can you make him rear up, and salute the crowd?"

"Yes, Ma'am. I can," she said. As she did, the crowd went wild.

"Wow! Oh, Folks, we have a real cowgirl here. She is going to be some rider as she gets older. What is her name?"

April dismounted the horse, patted its neck, and told the cowgirl, "April. My name is April D."

The announcer said, "Let's everyone give April D a round of applause for the horsemanship she displayed here today." And they did. They clapped, they whistled, and some threw their hats in the air. It was something April had never experienced before.

Then the cowgirl walked April back to where Johnnie was sitting, and the clown cowboys hoisted her up over the side to her seat. They congratulated Johnnie about having such a brave daughter.

"It's not my daughter," he said. "It's my . . ." and he looked at April, "sister. The cowgirl winked at him. "Little kids are chick magnets," he said. April did not have a clue what that meant. In her mind, body and soul, she was still riding that cowgirl's horse.

The rodeo was awesome. They saw their friend Travis bull ride. He rode a mangy red bull that twisted this way and that, and jumped higher than some horses jump that April had seen. That bull had beady black eyes, and he meant business. As hard as that bull tried to get Travis off, he could not. Travis went along each time the bull bucked, or twisted. He was soft on his back. It was really something, and Travis made his 8 seconds. He would go on to another show to increase his standings of winning prize money.

April remembered a time when she and her brother John were walking in the summertime. They spied four boys trying to coral a neighbor's bull, a white face Hereford, into a breeding box with an open top. That bull was slow and uncooperative. John looked at April who was staring at what was going on. They had a good view of sight standing on the hillside by that pasture. "Do you want to ride that bull?" John asked her.

"I sure do," she said. "But if we don't get there soon, that bull will be all played out." So off they scampered around the bend to the bottom of the pasture where the boys were.

There were four boys alright, all about John's age. "Hey John, can you help us put this bull in the breeding box?" they asked.

"I sure can. Well, we can if you stay out of the way. That bull does not know you, he knows us. We have helped here with him before. But if we do, my sister gets the first ride," he said.

"Oh, all right," they complained.

April ducked the fence boards and went into the pasture. She ran around in front of the bull, shaking a piece of plastic she found near the fence. It was clear with hole, but would work for what she intended. As she shook the plastic it made noise, and glistened in the sun. The bull shied away from her towards the box.

"Keep him coming," her brother called to her.

She did slowly from left to right saying, "Come on, move." and he went. When the bull got to the box area, John had removed his shirt, and he worked the bull on the right side. April had the left. As they walked towards the bull holding their articles, the bull wanting to get away from those shake things, went into the box. The other boys dropped the wood door, and John lifted the metal handle. He pulled it over to the L bar, locking the bull in. The front side had a door the same as the back.

Now that the bull was in place, they scrounged around for some twine to use to hold onto. They fished the twine up and around the bull seven or eight times. One would drop the twine down. The another on the ground would reach under the bull, grab the twine, and hand it back up to be dropped down again. All the while the bull munched on the tall grass that had grown because of nonuse of the breeding box.

John and April went up the steps of the box, telling the boys to move. They had the first ride. They were told to open the front door when he hollered ready. April climbed on first, holding her hands under the twine. John was second on, and he also dug his hand under the tight twine around April's small frame. "Are you ready?" he asked April. She shook her head yes, and John hollered, "Ready," and the front of the box opened.

The bull walked out slowly, sniffed the air and gave a little hop. Then he turned his head to look at them and bellowed three or four times. John kicked the bull hard in his ribs. The bull jumped twice, and John fell off. The bull then trotted down to the creek, splashing, and back up to the pasture. He jumped and bucked, and then that was it. April stayed on him, kicking him, and decided he was all played out. April slid off the bull's back, and walked backwards to make sure he would not charge her. She then ran to the fence rails. She and John left the boys standing there, wondering how they would get the bull back in the box. And how would they get the twine off of the bulls so they would not get in trouble. John and April laughed as they ran up the hill. They would have some explaining to do to Momma about how they got mud splatters all over their shirts.

Yes, April loved that rodeo. Johnnie bought her a hot dog and a soda. Later there was a clown walking around with a box in front of him. It had a rope that went from both sides of the box to around his neck. He would holler, "Peanuts, candy." When someone wanted some, he would stop, give them what they wanted, and make change from the apron bag in front of him that was tied around his waist. Johnnie wanted some peanuts, and the vendor said, "Two dollars, sir."

"Two dollars? I could buy a whole can for that price," Johnnie replied.

"Two dollars." the vendor said. Johnnie paid him, and then the peanut vendor, looking at April, handed her a bag of cotton candy for free. "That's for the champion riding cowgirl. Compliments of the house," and then he went on his way.

"If I had known you were going to get something free, I would not have paid for the peanuts," Johnnie said, and April laughed. "Give me some of your cotton candy, Toots. It had better taste good, At least let me get something free," he said.

The rodeo went on well into the night. April was getting sleepy, and asked Johnnie what time it was. "It's almost eight o'clock", he said, "Are you pooping out on me? Getting sleepy?"

"Yes, I am. Sorry," April replied.

"Okay, let's get out of here." Slowly they made their way down off of the bleachers to the ground. On ground level there was a lot going on. As they walked through, the cowgirl who lent April her horse came over to talk to the two of them.

"Hi, April D. So this is your big brother?" and the two of them stood there speechless.

"Yes, I am," said Johnnie. "And you are?"

"I am a cowgirl with the rodeo from Laredo, Texas. I am traveling with the rodeo. This is my job," the cowgirl said.

"Well, I don't suppose you would be interested in dinner or a date tonight?" Johnnie asked her.

"No, sorry. After the rodeo we all help each other to clean up, feed the animals, and then travel to another place for the weekend," she said.

"Well, you can't blame a guy for trying to get to know a beautiful cowgirl. Can you?" Johnnie asked her.

"No. I don't, but we cowgirls get hit on a lot. We are not showgirls. We are cowgirls, and do routines. It takes a lot of practice. We are down to earth, simple girls, who one day want a family of our own. But for now we get a chance to show our skills, make some money, and see the world," the cowgirl said.

"Funny, I never thought of it that way," Johnny admitted. And he asked her, "I travel through here and all over the state driving bus for a company. Will you tell me your name so if I come here again, I can ask to see you?"

"That would be fine, but I am only interested in friendship for now. My name is Jamie," she said. And soon others were calling her name to come and help them. "Sorry I have to go," she said as she left.

As they walked to the car, Johnnie said, "Win some, lose some. It's always the smart, decent girls I lose, Toots. Why is that?"

April looked at him with an eye that was sarcastic. "Maybe because you are a player. You are not interested in settling down. You are "out to sew oats," as my Momma used to say.

"Don't you know that a nice girl is like a filly?" April asked him.

"Filly? What is a filly?" Johnnie said.

April answered him, "a filly is a female horse, but a very young one. They can be a bit wild, but not all together wild. They are not always trusting of people. They shy away, and are sometimes hard to catch. They come willingly when they trust you. You never know what to expect from them. They are funny and full of spirit. That is what a filly is. If you are sincere, kind, and respect them, then they will eat out of your hand. They are just like single, young women. So take notes, and remember that, Goofy," April said to Johnnie.

Meeting Johnnie's Family

They drove for a while, and soon they came to a house. Johnnie got out, and banged on the side door that was in a breezeway connecting to the garage. Boom, boom, boom, he knocked. Soon a man came to the door and opened it. The two greeted each other with a hearty handshake and manly hug. "Dude, I didn't know you were in town," the man said.

"Just a stop overnight, and then I leave early in the morning," Johnnie said.

"Come in, come in. Honey, come out here. Johnnie is here." And Johnnie took April's hand pulling her along.

A very pretty woman with very long black hair came into the kitchen. She immediately came towards Johnnie with her arms open and hugged him like a bear. "Okay, Sis. Don't squish me to death," Johnnie said.

She let go, stood back, and looked at him. "You're getting older brother. What's with the wild hair?" she asked.

"I need a haircut. Okay? Don't bust on me just yet," Johnnie said, and he pulled April forward.

"Who is this?" the woman asked.

"This is April D. She is my date for the evening," Johnnie answered.

"Well, your taste has improved," the woman teased. "Hello. My name is Wendy. I am Johnnie's older sister. It's very nice of you to come and visit me. Do you want something to eat or drink?"

April thanked her, and said, "I would appreciate a glass of water. If it is not too much trouble."

The woman looked at Johnnie, her eyes getting bigger and bigger. "I like that. She has manners. I can see her doing you some good," and she laughed going to the refrigerator for a pitcher of cold water. She came to the table with a glass and the pitcher, and began to pour the cold water for April. "Are you sure you don't want something to eat sweetie? I have cookies and pudding," and she went to look through her cupboards. "I have chips, pretzels, and cheese crackers. Unless you'd like a sandwich?"

April looked at her trying to decide when Johnnie blurted out, "I'd like a beer and a sandwich, please?"

"Get it yourself," Wendy said to him.

"Sheesh, that's some real sisterly love, eh?" Johnny said looking at the man.

April said, "I would like a piece of fruit if you have some - a pear or an orange."

"Sure, sure I do. Well, this would certainly be an improvement for you. She's polite, has good manners, and knows what is good to eat," Wendy said to her brother who was intentional ignoring her.

They sat around the kitchen table talking about family members, catching Johnnie up on what was going on and happening in their town and with people they knew. This was of no interest to April, so she went over to Wendy and tapped on her shoulder saying, "Excuse me. Would you mind if I sat in the living room and slept?" Wendy's eyes got big again, and she laughed. "No. I certainly don't mind, but you should sleep in a bed." Then she used her fingers to squeeze April's belly.

Wendy got up, and the two of them walked down a hallway to a small bedroom. It was full of sewing material. "Don't mind the mess," she said. "I make a lot of clothing and quilts, so this is my sewing room. Sometimes when my husband is working long hours on the rigs, I come in here and sew. And when I am tired, I sleep in here too. I don't like sleeping in our big bed alone. I miss him too much."

Wendy fluffed the pillow and pulled the sheet down. "It's going to be a warm night. You won't need a blanket, but I will let it here in case you want one." Wendy made sure April was all tucked in, said Good night, and snapped off the light. She left a night light on that was in a plug high on the wall. April was asleep before she could think about what tomorrow would bring.

The morning came early for April as usual. She woke up, went to the bathroom quietly, and washed and brushed her hair to look presentable. She went into the kitchen and found a frying pan. In the refrigerator there were eggs and some ham slices. She thought she'd make breakfast for everyone.

First April set the table with four dishes, four glasses, and silverware that were clean in the dishwasher. Then she put the frying pan on the stove, and pushed a chair to the stove so she could reach the pan while cooking. She simmered the ham in a half cup of water on low. She found a can of orange juice in the freezer, and let it sit in a hot bowl of water. Then she took the pitcher in the sink, washed and dried it, and used that for the orange juice.

April did not want to cook the eggs until everyone was up. She turned the stove setting on warm for the ham. As she got down from the chair, she bumped open a cupboard. There she found pancake mix. All she needed was water.

April found another frying pan in the dishwasher, and put it on the front burner on low. She began to measure out pancake mix and water. She mixed it all up, and bumped up the heat on the pan for the pancakes. Then she sprinkled a little water on the pan to see if the water would skitter around, to tell if the pan was ready. It did, so she poured four small-sized pancakes out into the pan. Slowly the edges began to bubble. She waited, checked them, and then flipped them. Some got stuck on others, but she carefully separated them. April began to think she needed to make more noise in order to wake everyone, when Wendy came in the kitchen with her pajamas on. "Oh, wow. You cooked breakfast. How nice." She looked at all April had started, and said, "Good job, Kiddo. I am going to wake the guys up."

In no time April had twelve pancakes stacked up on a plate, and poured in the last of the batter. She put the orange Juice on the table and the ham slices on a plate taking them to the table Wendy came back in the kitchen. She was amazed at this little girl's skills, she was organized, and not afraid to cook. "Come on guys. The food will get cold," Wendy called. April shut off the burner to the pancake pan.

April put the last four pancakes on the plate. "Let me get that for you," Wendy said. She saw April standing on the chair, and might not be able to handle the large plate stacked with pancakes.

"Alright, but I could do it," April said to her.

"Oh, I don't doubt that. You put me to shame," Wendy said.

Soon the guys came out. Don, Wendy's husband, said, "What's all this? My wife never cooks breakfast."

Wendy slugged Don in the side saying, "I do too."

"When?" said Don. "When did you cook a hot breakfast, except oatmeal?"

Wendy answered him with a blushing face, "Last Christmas. Okay?"

They all sat down and dug in. Don said to Johnnie, "You can stop in anytime, if you bring her along," and they all laughed. Don then turned part way around to see what April was doing. "Come and sit down here, Kid, and eat."

April looked at Don from her chair height with one hand on her hip and the other hand holding a frying flipper, saying, "I am making eggs. How do you want yours, hard, soft and not runny, or scrambled?"

Don got out of his chair to watch her. "I like mine soft side. Can you do it?" he asked. April hit him with her flipper lightly and smiled. Soon she skillfully put the flat side of the tool under his egg and flipped it over. In less than a minute she flipped it back, and there sat a perfectly cooked soft-side egg.

"I married the wrong girl," Don said while carrying his eggs to the table. Everyone "oohed" at the sight of them, then they all wanted soft-sided eggs. Soon the whole carton of twelve eggs was cooked and sitting on a large plate beside the ham.

They all sat down. April looked at them beginning to dig in, and she said, "Wait. We didn't say prayers." They all stopped in midmotion, looking at each other, and then her. "Do you want me to say it?" she asked.

Don quickly said, "Yes. Go ahead. You say it."

So she did. "Dear Heavenly Father, we are so thankful for this good breakfast. We ask that you bless it so we can have strong bodies, be healthy, and that we can do what needs to be done this day. We love you, Heavenly Father, and we ask your spirit to be with us. Amen."

April lifted her head, and began to pick up a pancake. Everyone else was motionless, staring at her. "What's the matter? Isn't it any good? I thought you were hungry?" April asked.

"Oh, no. It's all good. We are all wondering how you learned to pray like that?"

"Oh, my Momma taught me," April answered as she chomped down her pancake smothered in syrup. They all ate until they felt like they were going to burst.

"I will remember this day for a long, long time," said Don. "That was the best breakfast I have ever had. You even cook better than going out, Miss April."

April beamed, and Don scooped her up making her giggle. "Oh, my tummy is too full," April said laughing.

Don sat down with April on his lap, and looked at Wendy. "We need some of these," he said to her.

"Oh, don't get any ideas. I don't think ours would be just like that. Some would be monkey wrenching in the garage with you and your bikes, and some would be glued to the TV," said Wendy.

Johnnie looked at the clock. It' was 8:00 a.m., "We must be back at the terminal by 10:00."

"You have an hour and a half." said Don.

"Yeah. I know, but I'd love to grab a shower. If I could? The next leg of the trip is going to be a long one."

"Go ahead, and get a shower. You don't need my permission," said Wendy. She tapped April on the leg, "Hey you want to go in our pool to rinse off, while hog boy is in the shower?"

"Okay," said April. "But I don't have a suit."

"I can fix that," said Wendy and she flipped April one of Don's t-shirts. April put it on, and in minutes was swimming in the pool. Twenty minutes later she was dressed and waiting for Johnnie.

April knew they would be leaving, and she might not see Wendy or Don again. So she went to Wendy, and told her, "Thank you for letting me stay overnight. The rodeo sure was a lot of fun, but I was tired. I hope I did not make too much of a mess in the kitchen making breakfast. I wanted to surprise everyone, and show my thanks," April said sincerely.

"Are you from Earth? Or did an alien drop you down to Earth?" Don asked, and Wendy threw a pillow at his head.

"Don't mind him. He's an old Fuddy Duddy."

"I am not," said Don. "But I have never met a kid that young who can cook and has such good manners."

April looked at him, and said. "You need to teach children by example. I watched my Momma cook many times, and often she would let me cook. Little by little I learned to make a lot of things, so I could cook for myself when she was in the barn.

"Barn?" asked Don.

"Yes, in the barn. My Momma was a dairy woman, and milked 300 cows every day and every night," said April.

120

"Now I know why she is like that. Her Momma worked, and was not lazy." Don said. He then threw a pillow at Wendy. Next thing April knew, Wendy rushed Don tackling him onto the couch.

About that time Johnnie came out, all spiffy and clean. "See. You let them alone for a few minutes, and they can't behave. They act worse than little children. I'm telling you, I am glad you have better manners, Miss April," he said.

Soon they were all saying good-bye and hugging each other including April. She and Johnnie got into the Mustang and off they flew. They got to the bus terminal in twenty minutes flat.

Johnnie showed April where to sit inside a small building. He soon came back to her with her belongings. His friend, who lent him the Mustang, came to where they were, and asked, "Did you wash it?"

Johnnie said sarcastically, "No. I didn't wash it. I did not have the time."

Then the friend slapped Johnnie on the back of the head, saying, "Some friend!" laughing as he went.

Johnnie checked his schedule, "Bus 45, that is our ride," he said. Next he took April to a long row of buses, and the third one was bus 45. He opened the door for her, and helped April up the steps to her seat. "Okay. You stay here. I am going to wait outside by the bus for our passengers to arrive.

April sat there and could see a long line of people approaching the bus. It was so exciting. She had butterflies in her tummy. Soon they would be on their way to New Mexico, and then California, finally! This had been a long, long journey on the bus and she was wanting so badly for all of this traveling, on and off the bus, to stop. April was excited and nervous to meet her Auntie in California for the first time. April wondered why her Momma never mentioned her. Momma never said they got a Christmas card, or pictures. April thought perhaps this Auntie was older, and did not bother much with anyone. Some people get like that.

Sometimes people say hurtful things, and then they don't talk to each other anymore. Sometimes people are mean. They take something, and promise to give it back with no intention of doing so. And that can cause people to stop contact with them.

April knew of a neighbor who sued another neighbor over a loan debt. It was to be paid, and never was. It was very ugly. They were brothers, and after the court suit they never spoke again. April thought that was plain stupid, the man who said he'd pay it back was the one who was in the wrong. He took advantage of his brother's kindness. Even though the brother who lent the money did try to visit his brother. He called and called, mailed many letters, but that man would never open his door, answer his calls, or write to him. How sad, how very, very sad.

It was spring in this part of the country, too. But the weather was much warmer than what she was used to in the eastern part of the country. The air-conditioning kicked in for the first time on their trip. "I am sweating," she said.

"Me, too," said Johnnie. "My butt and back are wet from sitting."

"You did not need to share that," April said grinning.

April liked Johnnie. She had him all wrong in the beginning. Johnnie definitely had a wall up with people. April thought he had been hurt somehow. And did not want to be close to anyone, unless he knew them well. Maybe that would be a good lesson for her. Maybe she should be more like that, than being so open - loving everyone, and trusting them right away.

Almost There

April thought about that for a while, and then shook her head. No. She knew that the Savior, Jesus Christ, loved everyone, no matter who they were - red, yellow, brown, black or white. He did not care if their eyes were slanted, had leprosy, or sick. Yes, everyone was to follow the Savior's example. April knew that the Savior loves everyone, but not their sins. So she felt that although she did judge Johnnie in the beginning, it was because she did not like his actions.

As they went along, it was more and more like country living. Cars were less, and April saw people riding horses or donkeys by the side of the road. Some of them had pack donkeys or mules piled high with blankets or pots, very high. She thought maybe they were going to a market to sell them. There was a market where she was from. There people brought in produce, baked good, antiques, clothing, shoes, and all sorts of things. Most likely that is what these people were doing. So she asked Johnnie, "Are they going to market?"

"Yeah, probably. There are a lot of markets. Some are on side streets, some inside and outside of buildings. You never can tell until you get to the spot, but I think that is where they are going," he answered her.

The bus groaned on and on. The ride was long, the sun was hot, and the air-conditioning was blowing full streams of cool air. April began to get sleepy. There was a movie playing, but she had no interest in a spy movie with shooting and stuff. So she curled up in her seat. She covered herself with the small blanket Barbara had given her, it had been on the bottom of her backpack. She was sure glad to have it.

Soon she was lost in sleep. Unconsciously she could hear the gears shift, people talking, and bits and pieces of talking from the movie. She was in and out of reality.

she was so tired, and in all it was a much needed rest. She dreamed she was at the rodeo, riding with the cowgirl. She loved seeing all the sights, and hearing the cowboys and cowgirls talk. April especially loved the rodeo clowns.

April saw many of them put their lives at risk saving riders by putting themselves in the direct line of the bulls. April was brave, but the bull she rode back home was nothing like these bulls. These bulls must be bred to become mean, rangy and wild. There is no way she wanted to be riding on or near bulls like that. At home they would be called rogue animals, and put down.

It was late in the afternoon when she awoke. "Hey, hey, hey. Good to see you again, Sunshine. You sure had a nice long snooze. That rodeo must have worn you out."

April sat up rubbing her eyes, and said, "No. I loved it. I loved every minute of it. I guess it was being up late and then up so early that made me tired."

Johnnie answered her back, "Yeah. I did not have lunch on the bus. That breakfast was really good, Toots. You can cook for me any day. What else do you know how to cook?"

"Oh, I make hot dogs, fish sticks, hamburgers, and meatballs. You know small things. I have never made big meals like a roast or meatloaf, but I know how from watching Momma."

"Dang. I could have a live-in cook," Johnnie laughed. He then told her they would be making a stop in New Mexico, for about two hours, and then loading to reach California.

April thought that soon she would be home, at her Aunt's house. She did not know what she looked like or even her name. She had no idea if she lived in a house, in a town, or in the country. If she livede in a trailer or a hut. April had no idea, and pondered these things.

And it really didn't matter to April where her Aunt's home was, so long as she loved her, and was kind to her. Oh, she did not expect love to jump out at her right at the beginning. But April just hoped as she obeyed and listened to her Aunt, everything would be alright. They would get along well until she would go back home.

Silently she said a prayer asking her Father in Heaven to help her, to keep her safe, and to lead her to good people who could love her and who she can love. April did not know anything, but she knew she had to trust God, and follow where he would want her to go.

There was no going back to where she had been and didn't know where back was anymore. April asked her Heavenly Father to watch over her family far, far away, and help her to find her way in life. To know what is right and wrong, and to choose what is right.

April wanted to please God and live safe, and she wanted to do good to all people. Most of all she asked that "He" provide a way for her to know what she should do in all ways. She promised to be brave, and to always ask him first in all ways. And she asked for forgiveness for hiding so many of her prayers. She was not afraid, but she did not want to offend anyone. She knew that some people did not believe in God, and they would be angry and offensive if she were to pray out loud. "They have their way, and I have mine," she thought. "And I am keeping mine. I need it, and I like it. I am not doing any harm to anyone or anything."

As the bus steadily rolled along, the land was like the desert - sandy, hot and dry. April thought about General Santa Anna and the Mexican army that we fought at the Alamo. April learned about this from her two brothers. They would read their history books to her. She asked Johnnie if they were going by that, and he said, "Nope. We are not." So she let that thought go. Maybe her Aunt could take her there.

Johnnie said that the northern part of New Mexico was lush with pine trees, very pretty, much like the Poconos in Pennsylvania. April was somewhat familiar with that, as she had been through that area with her family. It had many kinds of leafy trees and pine trees that were in dense woods. She remembered a hike that her family went on in the Poconos.

Then the bus began to slow down. It was a check point by the police. Johnnie slowed to a crawl. He knew he would not make the scheduled time this way, but he also knew he had to comply with the police. He grabbed the mic, "No problems, Folks. It's just a check point. Sit still, and we will be through this in no time," Then he put the mic back in its holder.

One by one, the police looked at the cars. Some opened the car doors and looked inside. Only one was detained and the police had that truck pull over. They were looking at papers and whatever as the bus passed them.

The bus stopped, and Johnnie used his leaver to open the bus doors. A policeman stepped up on the bus, looking at all of the passengers. The policeman walked partway back on the bus, hitting his hand with a bat-like stick. He looked at several of the passengers' passports or papers. He came back, and tapped April on her back. April looked up at him, and smiled the most pleasant smile she could muster under such frightening instance. "Where are her parents?" he asked Johnnie.

Johnnie said, "She is my cousin. That is why she is sitting up front near me. She is going to our Aunt's home in California. I volunteered this leg of the trip to be with her, to make sure she reached our Aunt's home safely." The police officer was satisfied with Johnnie's answer. Then he tipped his hat forward to Johnnie and April, and got off the bus.

Within ten minutes of the officer disappearing in the crowd, the passengers on our bus began to clap their hands, and yell to Johnnie, "Good man, John boy." They were all happy that April was not taken off of the bus. For April, she was still sitting very still. That scared her stiff.

Johnnie could have lost his job, and she may have been detained for, gosh, who knows how long.

"Hey, Toots," Johnnie said to her. "Stop fretting, it's over. We are pulling out in a few minutes, and will be back on schedule in no time."

"But you put yourself at risk for me," April said.

"Yep, I did. And I would do it again, one hundred times if asked. It is not his or anyone else's business where you are going. It's your ticket, and it is paid for. On our bus we are taking good care of you, and we do not need their approval. That is how it is here and now. So in less than ten minutes we will be out of here, and on our way." And by the look on his face, April knew he meant what he said.

Sure enough in ten minutes the bus they were on, was flagged out, and back onto the highway. They were soon speeding along heading into California. "I told you. Didn't I?" Johnnie said to her watching her in his mirror. He was smiling, and April blew him a kiss. "Awe! You are sweet on me. Are ya?" he asked her.

April said, "Who wouldn't be? You saved me, and I owe you big time."

"Forget it." he said. "That is who I am, and what I am about. On my job I protect my passengers. And you, Kiddo, you have become like a sister to me," and he winked at her.

As they traveled on, Johnnie picked up the mic again. "Folks, here is a question for you all to think about. It's 11:00 a.m., and I can stop for an early lunch, or push through. I would rather push through to another spot. I also think there are more traps like the last one. If we go another hundred miles, we will be in California about 2:00 p.m. and we can stop there for something to eat, and stretch your legs. Most of you get off near there. It's up to you, stop or go.

There was a commotion with passengers talking about what to do. Soon a man said, "The majority of us would rather you push through, and we can stop to eat about

2:00 p.m. Then most of us will leave since we are near that area anyway." So that was what the bus majority decided to do, and Johnnie was happy. He wanted to put all the check points behind him with as much distance as possible.

There was a woman who came around passing out candy to the passengers. She gave a piece to everyone. She said she did not want to take it along with her when she got off. So as she headed back to her seat, April leaned forward and tossed the candy to Johnnie. He grinned. "How did you know?" he said. April just smiled at him.

As promised, around 2:00 p.m. the bus pulled into a nice place to eat. As the passengers got off, Johnnie looked at April, and said, "Well, Toots, one more stop, and you are home free."

April looked at Johnnie and said, "I am not sure how to feel about that. I don't know where I am going, or what my Aunt looks like. But I have to go, and I will be brave."

Johnnie said, "Let's get something to eat."

They were the last to enter the restaurant. After being seated, April went to wash up in the bathroom, as did Johnnie. They both arrived at their table at the same time. Johnnie stopped her, pulled out her chair, and pushed her in toward the table. April smiled at him. Johnnie could be quite the gentleman when he wanted to be.

They each had a steak salad, and they shared a plate of French fries. They both said it was all very good. On the way out Johnnie got a few snacks. And when on the bus he handed them to April. "Here, Kid. This is for you in case your Aunt is late."

The bus rumbled to a start. Johnnie called it a piece of crap, and he headed back out on the road. "Man, I was nuts to take this route. I have been driving now for eleven days straight, and I need some time off. The only good thing that happened to me on this trip is you, Toots."

April was glad she made someone happy. Within the next forty-five minutes was the stop for many of the passengers. The bus groaned to a stop with brakes squeaking. "Man, they have got to look at this piece of garbage. I'd like to know why I get all the older buses that are so near breaking down. I end up grinding my teeth." He got off the bus, and asked April if she wanted to get off too. She shook her head "no".

April sat in her seat beginning to feel dread, like she was all alone. And it would be like this for a long time, maybe forever. April knew she should not cry, to be brave, and she took a deep breath several times to push that feeling away. So she stood up, hollered, slapped her face, and began to do jumping jacks to get her thoughts off of thinking like that.

After two hundred jumping jacks, April was out of breath and panting. She sat down, pulled out a bottle of water that was given to her, and took a long drink. "I'll be alright," she said to herself, and April believed it with all her heart. She sat there wondering what in the world was going to happen next? Where was she going? She was in a state of confusion, unable to make heads or tails.

April was the only person on the bus. Johnnie came back in a little while, thumping up the steps. April could tell he was upset. "Well, Toots. It's you, me, and this pile of tin. We are stuck with it. I am to deliver you to your stop, and then return to this dive to get another bus. This one has had it. You'd think they would give me another bus now for safety's sake, but, oh no, old Johnnie Boy can do anything. He will get this bucket of tin to keep going to take you to your stop and come back. I am a miracle worker! That's what I am, a miracle worker of metal and machinery." Johnnie's face was red.

April looked at Johnnie, and felt a bit sorry for him. He stared at her, just waiting for a response. "Complaining will not make it any better." she said. "Put on your big boy pants, and deal with it," April said. Johnnie laughed, and soon the both of them were laughing. Johnnie looked at her. April sure had a way of making him see things in a different way.

Johnnie turned the ignition, and the bus rattled to a start. The old bus shuttered as it creaked and crawled out of the alleyway back onto the road. "Okay. Let 'er rip." Johnnie yelled. He pressed the gas pedal to the floor, and they were soon going forty-five miles per hour. Johnnie just sat there steering while shaking his head.

April did not know about cars, and she did not want to know. She felt sorry for Johnnie, but felt he could do what his company asked of him. It always makes things worse when nothing seems to go right, and then there is someone complaining. Just do what you have to do, and in time it will all work out. That is what her Momma always told her. It's not the end of the world.

They traveled on for another half hour or so. Soon Johnnie steered the bus onto another post for the bus company. The road was dirt and the bus shook from side to side as it crawled its way to the end of the driveway. As the bus eased into the remote outpost bus station, the bus' brakes screeched to a halt. Then Johnnie turned to his right to adjust his cap, and quickly peeked into his mirror. Johnnie looked at April and said, "Well. Last stop, Cupcake."

My Destination

"This looks like your kind of place. It's not over-populated, and I am sure there are ranches and horses all around here." April stood up, put on her backpack, and carried her tiger in her right hand and her suitcase in her left. There was no hurry to get off of the bus, she was the last passenger.

Slowly April walked up to exit the bus when Johnnie spoke to her. He tapped her on the shoulder, and April turned to look at him. April was already feeling fearful. Tears were beginning to well up in her eyes.

"Don't cry, Toots. Maybe your Auntie does not have a telephone. I am sure someone will come for you. You stay at the bus station. Make them throw you out, but don't leave it. This is where your Auntie will come to find you. Here . . ." and Johnnie scribbled down something on a paper and put the paper in her hand. "This is my phone number. It is toll free, meaning you can call me from anywhere, a pay phone or someone's house phone, and it will not cost them or you're a dime. Call me if no one comes. And either I will come and get you or have someone pick you up and bring you to me. I know Fred and I can get you anywhere you need to go."

April leaned forward and kissed Johnnie's cheek. He was quite taken aback, and was quiet and very solemn. "Hey, Cupcake, you take care, and remember what I told you," he reached for her. Then gave April a big hug.

April walked down the platform and steps to the ground. There was no one around. There was not one car, not one bicycle. It was not late. April guessed it was about 3:00 in the afternoon. But this area sure looked desolate from where April stood.

The bus station was little more than a wooden building, with a brick bottom. It was similar to a post office near where April was from. All except for the white sign across the top of the door which read BUS STATION. April walked up the cement steps to the front screen door. Taking ahold of the handle, she walked inside. There was a very pretty woman standing behind the counter who watched her.

April stood in front of the counter on her tippy toes and said, "Excuse me."

"How can I help you sugar?" a woman asked her.

No one ever called April that before. April looked at the woman, and asked, "Is this Fresno and is there someone waiting here?"

"Why yes, it is. Well, sort of," replied the woman. "Fresno is the name of the bus stop, but the town name is Caruthers, but there is no one waiting in here."

April did not totally understand, and she did not want to volunteer any information. She just said, "Thank you," turned around, and walked back out the door. The bus had already left, and April stood there feeling very alone.

April looked all around her. There were farm fields as wide and as far as you could see. The weather was not hot, but it was sticky. She could see workers mopping their heads with rags. April stepped down from the porch area onto the cement steps and began to walk towards those fields. There were many people out there picking what looked like onions, big fat long-stringed onions. April saw a little girl walking close to her Mother in the dirt rows while the Momma was lifting onions out of the dirt, shaking them free from the soil, and putting the onions into a basket. When that basket was full, a little further up the row line there was another basket. If the woman needed a basket to fill, the little girl would run and get one for her Mother.

April remembered working like that, not picking onions, but potatoes. The flatbed truck came very early in the morning to pick them all up in front of their farmhouse. It was chilly outside. April's Momma dressed her in a dress, with her coat and cap. April was very cold sitting there on the back of that flatbed truck as it drove along. Her brother came, and sat down beside her. "Are you cold?" he asked her. April nodded her head "yes". At that her brother took off his coat. He put his right arm in the right sleeve and April's left arm in the left sleeve. Then he would pull them close together to share the warmth inside both jackets. Yes, April remembered.